ADULT LOVERS

Prologue

Chloes hands shook as she pushed on the new email. Another customer show demand for her cam demonstrating persona, Cinnamon. She wasnt accustomed to it yet. Indeed, even following a month and a half new demands made her shake. She had two ordinary customers who mentioned shows and photograph sets, however all the other things was inconsistent. Another solicitation wasnt strange.

His username made Chloe grunt: CallMeSir. Truly? She had met a couple wannabe doms somewhat recently. They werent any great whatsoever. Few people were hot on talk, they needed her to be provocative without them accomplishing any work.

She pushed answer to the email.

All things considered, Sir, before we meet in private we ought to get to know one another. I am Cinnamon, Im 26, Im a Libra. My beloved artist is Lana Del Ray. I appreciate pineapple on my pizza, or chicken and feta cheddar. In my extra time, haha who I am joking? I dont have spare time. At the point when I have time I like to see my companions. Ive never been accommodating to anybody, however for the perfect individual I would be intrigued.

She hit send and opened her photograph altering system to complete the series of photographs shed taken for a customer.

A notice sprung up around 20 minutes after the fact.

Indeed, Cinnamon, Id like to improve. Be that as it may, in the event that you get excessively sassy, I wont wonder whether or not to hit you. Im 28, and my google search let me know Im an Aquarius. I likewise like elective music, Lana Del Ray has an interesting style. Marry need to arrange separate pizza as Im certain none of those things go on genuine pizza. I have companions I like to invest energy with. I was as of late unloaded so Ive been having a miserable outlook on connections, which is the reason Im here. I really want somebody to make me come. I utilized an arbitrary generator to pick my name, however a little control may be entertaining. Whats your cherished sex toy?

Chloe expanded at the screen. Most loved sex toy? He was unquestionably more dull that her standard customers. He knew what he needed, and he wasnt hesitant to inquire. Great initial feeling. She grinned as she answered. A couple coy messages and they put it down on the calendar for two days from now. He additionally requested a couple photographs to hold him over and she sent them after he paid. She needed to step away to take them; he needed her in accommodating stances.

Chloe stomach rippled as she wearing ribbon for her first show with the strange man she had been messaging with. Indeed, she spent a huge piece of two days sitting tight for and reacting to his messages. They had discussed torment and delight finally. He purchased more photographs of her wearing a bunch of areola clips and he mentioned a video of her stroking off.

She pulled at Cinnamon; her change self image, the piece of her who adored the consideration, who cherished sex, adored exchanging herself for cash. While she painted her face, she felt Cinnamon dominate. The vacillate changed from nerves to fervor and excitement.

Throughout the most recent two days she traded just about fifty messages with her new customer. Around evening time shed have a face and voice to connect to her dreams.

At her PC, she turned on her camera and paused. He was in visit yet no video. She waved and pantomimed blowing a kiss. Hi Sir. Ive been invigorated for this second.

CallMeSir: Im having some specialized hardships. My camera and mic arent working. Sick need to type my side.

Cinnamons grin floundered briefly. She skiped in her seat. Obviously, Sir. Whatever works for you. I was expecting to see you.

CallMeSir: Whys that?

She gave him a hesitant grin, rippling her lashes. Your words have enlivened a couple dreams.

CallMeSir: Oh, have you been underhanded? I need you to snatch the yield you showed me and rebuff yourself?

Cinnamon gazed at the screen. He said he needed to hurt her, yet she didnt anticipate that it should be this evening. Nor did she hope to be turned on by the thought. Shed never been into torment, yet nobody had asked her all things considered.

She needed to burrow through her toy box to observe the harvest she prodded him with in a reward picture. Holding it up, she raised her foreheads. Where?

CallMeSir: Your thighs. Tip the camera so I can see you turn your skin red.

She adhered to his guidelines, trusting her sweat-soaked palms didnt make her drop the yield. First shows were never this simple, never moved this quick. This wasnt his first time with a model, or he knew what he needed. Regardless, she slapped her thighs with the yield until he stopped her with his words.

CallMeSir: Are you wet?

She gestured, gnawing her lip. So ridiculously wet. Her voice shuddered as she talked. Nerves, she wasnt used to being open with regards to the condition of her pussy. Not yet, she was improving. Zero in on the customer.

CallMeSir: Show me. Also, put the braces on your areolas.

Cinnamon peeled off her lacey outfit and whimpered into the camera when the clasps shut on her areolas. Then, at that point, she showed him how her exposed pussy lips sparkled with her craving, after she clandestinely scoured it over herself. She ought to talk, however she couldnt think about something damn other than, Please let me come yet she didnt ask. Not yet.

CallMeSir: Touch your clit Cinnamon. Rub it and make yourself come while I jerk off.

She squeezed her fingers to her clit, attempting to envision what he resembled watching her from some obscure area. Simply being watched was sufficiently hot, she scoured her clit, somebody who might be listening was scouring himself to her body rotating in her seat.

Her pleasure worked at lightning speed, energizing her as she soared to climax. She couldnt help groaning, as the satisfaction snapped through her body. Cinnamons body went careless against the seat, as she hung tight for herself to get back to business as usual.

CallMeSir: Jesus, I havent come that hard in a very long time.

What's more, they had done as nearly nothing, minimal prodding, little being a tease, or toys. A little aggravation, a ton of delight.

Me not one or the other, Sir. Im happy I could satisfy your cravings around evening time.

CallMeSir: Kneel for me before I go.

You have ten additional minutes.

CallMeSir: You were awesome. Stoop like a decent young lady. Allow me just to see you submitting to me. So ridiculously lovely.

Cinnamon slid to her knees on the floor so the camera could see her. She took a gander at the screen, sitting tight for his next guidelines. At whatever point you need me to be your acceptable young lady, let me know, sir.

CallMeSir: Ill need that again soon Cinnamon. You are an excellent young lady. Rest soundly.

CallMeSir has logged off.

Chloe wound down the camera without lifting herself from the floor. This was the new typical. Taking her garments off for outsiders, coming for them, and getting compensated.

Night One

I turned into a cam young lady a couple of months prior when I was falling short on reserves. My lease was expanded, my work cut my extra time, and I didnt know about any fast choices other than asking my companions for cash. I couldnt take the shame, so I turned on my webcam, found a site that compensated fairly, and made it work.

Im taking a gander at my choices. A superior paying position, less expensive spot, stripping for outsiders on the web as my everyday work. Cam work pays all around ok, in addition to the climaxes. I dread what I would tell my loved ones.

This evening an ordinary has mentioned a private show. His username is CallMeSir, however the primary private show we did he advised me to call him TJ. I dont know TJ outside this domain. He doesnt use voice, as different regulars. He types what he needs from me. It makes it more hard to follow orders since I must be near the screen to peruse his words. However, we make it work.

I have my hair done in waves. TJ commended on my hair a couple of times. In the mirror, I put on my most splendid red lipstick, my red push up bra, and fancy red underwear. He prefers trim.

I have my crate of toys close by. I organized it before in the manner TJ ordinarily trains me to utilize the toys. Areola braces, paddle, this lube with menthol he taught me to purchase that makes my clit or areolas more touchy, and the vibrating dildo. There are more dildos in another container, butt plugs, in the event he has another solicitation.

I sign on and test my cam and mic. I orchestrate myself in a frown and watch the screen.

CallMeSir has signed on.

It starts.

Hi TJ. How are you?

CallMeSir: Hello, Cinnamon. Im tired in the wake of a monotonous day. How are you?

Mmm. Im OK. Work was not much. I contemplated you from morning 'til night. Considering what you would cause me to do this evening. I slide my forefinger between my lips and suck on it, giving him a bashful look.

CallMeSir: I contemplated you as well. I just went to the restroom once to jerk off. What might be said about you?

I didnt have time. In any case, that is not hot. My undies were drenched the entire day, yet I didnt need to squander a climax at work. I needed to save it for you.

CallMeSir: I think that is better. I like the possibility of you nervous the entire day while you consider me.

Ive made him a symbol in my mind. Hes presumably not at all like I envision. Yet, I see him mysterious yet attractive. Penetrating green eyes. Or then again blue. Or then again dull profound brown. So the eyes change contingent upon the mind-set. He has that messy look that is hot. It would scratch my internal thighs.

I need to continue to converse with him. I need to pose him individual inquiries. Yet, when I have tried things out, hes been equivocal. I realize he has an option to be mysterious, yet we two or three times each week, to some degree once in private each week, and afterward he joins my public shows here and there. Yet, it comes up short on the closeness of our private meetings. Furthermore, the manner in which he causes me to feel in them. Ive done the cam shows for a five months however just know TJ for around two months, Im dependent. I anticipate them much more than I ought to. I utilize his words, his directions each time I contact myself.

Would it be a good idea for us to get everything rolling? I shouldnt be so obtuse. Possibly I should continue to be a tease until he inquires.

CallMeSir: I love the red lipstick. Id like to see your lips folded over my dick.

Id like to have your dick in my mouth. Pay attention to you groan while I utilize my tongue on you.

CallMeSir: I bet you get all messy when you suck dick.

I do. I love a decent messy dick sucking meeting.

CallMeSir: Get that purple dildo, the one with the veins, practically like a genuine dick. Its greater than most folks, however show me.

However, youre greater than most folks. I curve to my toy box close to me and open the hook on top. He cannot see my smile. Each person thinks they are the greatest and best.

I observe the dildo he demands and fly back onto the screen with it. I squirm my hand and make it flop around with a smile.

CallMeSir: Youre being a whelp around evening time as of now, Cinnamon. I may need to beat you.

Indeed I am greater than most folks.

I try not to shake my head. Anything you desire to accept, daylight. Its his cash.

I stroke my hand along the phony dick. I put on my best provocative voice. TJ, you have the greatest dick Ive seen. I dont know whether I can deal with somebody this large.

CallMeSir: Youll take it, my skanky young lady. Presently suck on the tip.

I part my lips and suck on the top of the dick. I imagine its human, warm, its appended to the tall, dim, attractive man and hes remaining above me while I stroke him, while I taste him.

One eye is on the screen, standing by additional guidance.

CallMeSir: Take it more profound. Show me how profound you can get.

He knows its not profound. However, he enjoys making me gag on it. My debilitated charlatan. I press my tongue down on the floor of my mouth and push it profound until I cannot deal with it. I swallow hard, yet my gag kicks in.

CallMeSir: I think that is more profound than last time. I need you to rehearse for the following week once a day hold it as profound as possible however long you can. If you improve, there will be a tip.

I gesture, looking directly at the camera, my mouth loaded with purple dick. Ideally straight at him. I envision they are dull this evening. Dull and agonizing.

CallMeSir: Get messy down on it. Allow me to see your spit run down your jaw.

I utilize my tongue around his dick, slackening my lips enough so he can see my tongue working the tissue. Spit dribbles from my mouth down my jawline. I battle to prevent myself from cleaning it away, rather I constrain myself to push more out.

CallMeSir: Good young lady. Id fill your mouth with my come and watch it dribble down your jawline. Down your chest. If I had sufficient the means to purchase a night with you Id cover you in my come. Take the dildo out and let me know if youd like that.

From him? Presumably.

Indeed, Sir. Id like to be loaded up with your come, canvassed in it.

My pussy is wet and jolted. I need to contact myself.

CallMeSir: Youre such a messy young lady. After I filled your mouth, Id push you on the bed and beat your butt red.

This is the part he appreciates most. Making me hurt myself.

No, its him harming me. Im his intermediary.

Would it be advisable for me to get the oar? I chomp my base lip.

CallMeSir: Let me see your underwear first.

I tip the cam so it shows my clothing. I stand up and turn all around so he can see them. Is it accurate to say that he is grinning? Does he like them? I got them for you.

My face warms, humiliated in light of the fact that its valid. I considered him while I selected seven new matches of underwear at the unmentionables store. One for every evening. If you wear similar undies time after time, the regulars get on it and grumble. Fuckers. Be that as it may, for TJ, Id do anything to satisfy him.

CallMeSir: Red is my new most loved shading. The shade of your skin after Im done beating it.

A groan gets away from me. I slap my hand over my mouth.

CallMeSir: Dont conceal your groans. I need to hear them all.

Sit on the seat and show me how wet your underwear are. Have you destroyed them as of now?

I chomp at the tip of my finger and gesture, with an underhanded grin, the young lady trapped in the treat container. Indeed, Sir. Im wet.

CallMeSir: Show me how wet. Sit in your seat and put your feet on the seat, spread your legs and show my your wet underwear.

I sit and change the camera so its focused in on my groin. Whenever I first did this I figured I may bite the dust. However, presently its the same old thing. Theres a little moist fix.

CallMeSir: You arent drenched at this point. Take them off and show me within.

The fix inside my clothing is greater. I hold the red trim close so he can examine. We havent done what's necessary to get me splashed. Maybe after the hitting.

CallMeSir: Not terrible from sucking a phony dick on a camera. You like being a trouble maker.

I do TJ. I like being your miscreant. I never would do these things in the event that you didnt inquire. My voice is a murmur, I incline nearer to the mic so he can hear me. However, that is troublesome. Im admitting realities, however I dont know whether he knows its reality. It very well may be a persona Im playing for him. Its not, yet he might trust that. All cam young ladies have a persona. I do as well, yet with TJ its unique.

CallMeSir: I know. That is the reason you are my top pick. Get the wooden oar. I wish I could be there in your room, twist you over the seat and punish you like you merit.

I set my underwear on the PC work area and recover the wooden oar. Not what I envisioned he would need, but rather he generally surpasses my assumptions.

CallMeSir: I may need to work all the more extra time to manage the cost of more private meetings with you. I could purchase your time and hush up about all of you.

I slap the oar against my internal arm, it doesnt hurt, simply makes a slap strong.

CallMeSir: Do you have the areola braces on?

I shake my head. No, Sir. I was hanging tight for your authorization.

CallMeSir: Take off your bra and put them on. Draw near to the cam so I can perceive how close they are.

I move close, my areola fills the screen and I cut it around the delicate stub. Fuck. I nibble my base lip until the underlying aggravation blurs. The glimmer of talk gets my attention as I move to the subsequent side.

CallMeSir: For the other one, let me see your face.

I sit in the seat and set up the subsequent clip. I ensure Im investigating the camera before I discharge it against my skin. The aggravation shoots through me, making me murmur.

CallMeSir: Some ladies can get off from simply their areolas.

Im more delicate I think than normal, yet not so much. I really want my clit contacted to get off. If by some stroke of good luck it were just simple.

CallMeSir: Noted. Slap that oar against your thighs. Make it hurt.

I slap it against my thighs, three blows each, hard enough to make my mouth drop open. Great? I ask in a tight voice.

CallMeSir: adequately good. Stand up, pivot, and back rub your butt with two hands. Warm up the muscle. Two or three minutes is acceptable. Then, at that point, pivot for more guidance.

I put the oar away and pivot. I get my butt with two hands and hold as profound into the tissue as I can. Following two minutes passes, I spin around to see his next words.

CallMeSir: Warm yourself with the oar. You can pivot each ten beats to check in.

I get the oar. Its new to me. He got it for me, and we havent utilized ithowever. We utilized other lighter devices, yet this was a unique request. I rub a finger over my lip while gazing into the camera while I track down a decent grasp on the oar.

My nerves are stewing with a blend of excitement and nervousness.

CallMeSir: Do you need to do this?

My dithering is observable. Indeed, Sir.

CallMeSir: If you dont need to we can accomplish something different.

Its not the aggravation keeping me down. I like the aggravation. Im apprehensive I wont satisfy your hopes.

Theres no answer for quite a long time. I go after the mouse, prepared to invigorate the page on the off chance that something froze up. In any case, the three dabs that let me know hes answering spring up. I slap the oar against my hip until his answer comes up.

CallMeSir: You generally surpass my assumptions. Take the initial ten lethargic, consistent. Its a warm up.

Ive gained such a huge amount from him regarding where the lines of agony and delight obscure. He talks in verse, however the dirtiest screwing verse youve read. He can stimulate me with a couple of keystrokes. Accommodation to him isn't only for the cash any longer. Its him. Its TJ. Its my Sir.

I cannot let him know any of that, I just pivot and slap my butt multiple times. I return to him.

CallMeSir: Ten more.

Ten, becomes twenty. He teaches me to hit more enthusiastically every time until it harms. I need to cry on myself, to hurt, to show him the amount I need to satisfy him with my red skin. However, that self-conservation kicks in. I wonder where he resides. If I could see him. If I could allow him to slap me adequately hard to please us both.

No, taking this off the web is excessively perilous. He could be a chronic executioner, or something to that effect. I dont need to demolish this dream. Meeting me may demolish his dream of me. A piece of the energy comes from the dream.

I shout out for the last ten. My skin is red, I can see it in the screen behind me. My muscles will be sore tomorrow from standing firm on the situation and the unpleasant treatment of my butt. Also, I would delight in it. It will be the best screwing day of all time.

CallMeSir: Thats enough. How would you feel?

I remain there gazing at the screen. The camera point cuts off my head. Great. A piece trippy.

CallMeSir: Move the cam. I need to see your face. Is it accurate to say that you are turned on?

I understand Im breathing weighty as I move the cam back to my face. Am I turned on? I shut my eyes and tune into my body. I dont know. It was overpowering for me. That was exceptional.

CallMeSir: It was. Possibly we should stop here.

No! Oh no. I snatch my seat and sit. I pull my tone back. Nobody has come at this point.

CallMeSir: Thats valid. However, im OK. That meeting gave me enough for seven days of masturbatory feed.

I frown. You dont need to see me come?

CallMeSir: I need to ensure you are alright before my narrow minded longings.

Gracious. Indeed, I need to come. I need to make you come while you watch me.

CallMeSir: I need that. I need to watch you screw yourself with that purple dildo.

I snatch the dildo and a container of ointment from my crate, test my sanity up and take a gander at the screen. Would you be able to see me?

CallMeSir: I can. In any case, move back so I can see your hot twat and face.

Let me know when. I edge in reverse until he gives the word.

CallMeSir: Im happy you let your hair develop out a bit. Dont be annoyed, I dont like an uncovered pussy.

I grin as I rub the dildo against my cut. Sick recollect that. Im going to imagine this is your dick scouring against me. Marry lie on my bed, on my silk sheets and youd be over me, scouring your dick against my cut, prodding me.

CallMeSir: I have my dick in my grasp, and Ill envision that also. Id like to get smooth from your pussy.

Get the dildo wet in your pussy then, at that point, draw it off.

I utilize my fingers to part my lips and prod the head into my opening. Together they make a slurping sound. I lift the purple dick to my lips and draw my juice off. Its great, yet I wish it was my pussy served from your genuine dick.

I push the dildo inside my twat and push it gradually. Youd screw me delayed for a couple of moments, genuine sluggish, prodding me. Then, at that point, push your dick in my mouth and our preferences would blend. A wonderful new formula.

CallMeSir: goodness indeed, Cinnamon. Screw yourself with the dildo.

I push the dick quicker. Wish it was TJ drilling me. His mouth covering mine to swallow my groans. I let them out, uproarious and glad.

My excitement mounts to the limit. I cannot get off this way. I cannot emerge out of entrance alone. A moan gets away from my mouth. I want a vibrator to come. Would you care if I switch?

CallMeSir: Grab whatever you want. Im close. Im envisioning pulling on your areola cinches and making you shout my name. Then, at that point, Id play your clit like my guitar.

He plays guitar? Great to know. I make a note and throw the dildo on a towel on the floor in any case they get feline hair on them.

I get my beloved vibrator. Its an extravagant one that has 1,000,000 vibration settings. I flip through to find one that is solid and consistent. I need to get off as quick as could really be expected.

CallMeSir: Make yourself come for me, my lovely whore.

I ensure my pussy is in the camera view before I spread my twat lips and press the vibrating silicone against my clit. Its murmur charges each nerve in my body. I shut my eyes and envision my mysterious yet attractive TJ between my legs, licking my pussy like its hes starved for it. His eyes are dim on mine as he eats up me.

The shaking begins from my clit and spreads through my hips and thighs. I utilize one hand to hold the seat as the climax surpasses me.

My mouth drops open. TJ. Fuck, yes. Im coming so mind-blowingly hard.

The climax leaves me limp in my seat.

The screen is blazing, so I open my eyes.

CallMeSir: I came as well. Screw that was hot.

Beneficial thing I thought ahead and brought a towel around evening time.

Is it true that you are alright?

Im OK. You didnt kill me. Beneficial thing I dont have plans to move after youre finished with me.

CallMeSir: That great? It looked great.

It was screwing stunning, TJ. You make me come better compared to anybody.

CallMeSir: Good. Im happy. I wish I could take you to bed, and nestle you every night.

Then, at that point, wake me with more incredible sex, correct? This dream sounds way better compared to it ought to.

CallMeSir: Yes! :) Before I go I need to watch your face when you remove your areola clasps. Youve been wearing them a long-lasting around evening time, ought to be a decent one.

Youre a savage. I give a phony snarl.

CallMeSir: Ive been told its my best quality.

Hes a lot better than he gives himself credit for, yet he appreciates seeing me in torment. I plant my feet on the floor and snatch the right clip and delivery it. Agony shoots through my body as the blood surges back in. I drop the clasp and get my bosom as the air whooshes out of me.

CallMeSir: I never worn out on watching your face when you take them off.

I scowl at the screen, then, at that point, strip the second away. Fuck, fuck, fuck. My hand cups my bosom and my palm attempts to mitigate, however just aggravates. Yet, in under a moment the aggravation melts away and vanishes into the ethos of my recollections.

Screw that damages like damnation. I love it before you inquire. Im nearly stirred once more. I duck my head as my face warms.

CallMeSir: Im happy you had a goodbye. So did I. Youre a decent young lady. You merit a prize. We will talk again soon.

Goodbye, Sir.

He logs off, then, at that point, I close my PC down. I clean my toys and pack them away. At the point when I open the room entryway, the feline sneaks in and twists up on the finish of my bed. Without dressing, I slide into my silk sheets. An extravagance I oversaw last week with additional tips from the cam work.

My telephone blares from the end table and I really look at it. Email, a tip. My eyes enlarged. A major tip from TJ. With the message, Dont fail to remember your profound throat practice.

I wont. Sick email him toward the beginning of the day about it. Furthermore, regularly until we have another private show. My body is as yet humming. I snatch my wand from the end table and press it between my legs, carrying myself to climax once more, recollecting every one of the things he said and I did this evening.

This is awful. Im stuck between a rock and a hard place. Im dependent on this man. Furthermore, his honeyed words and the manner in which he causes me to feel, the things he does to me. Its to an extreme, excessively quick, excessively unusual.

Night Two

I lean back in my chair and look around the bar. It's Saturday, but it's early evening so there aren't too many people here yet. I pick at the corner of the label on my beer. The woman across from me laughs at her own joke.

I am dying. My dream girl in front of me and I cannot touch her. At least I can't embrace her the way I want.

"I need to get home," she says. My best friend, Chloe tips the rest of her beer into her mouth. I focus on the soft skin of her throat. What would it feel like under my lips?

I can't see anything besides her. We might was well be alone instead of at a table in a busy bar. Might be good we aren't alone. If we were, I would start with a brush across the back of her hands and end with me buried inside her. She'd thrash around, moaning while I make her come.

"What are you doing?"

"I have work to catch up on." She wrinkles her nose.

I know it's a lie. I know what she really does. By day she's Chloe, a funny cute underappreciated secretary. By night, she's Cinnamon, a temptress and masochist.

She doesn't know when she gets home, the money she makes will be from me. I stumbled upon her cam show one horny, lonely night. I don't know why she does cam work. Does she like it? Does she need the money?

I signed up for one of her private spots, intending it to be a quick tease and I'd go back to my regular woman. Cinnamon/Chloe, whoever she is, differs from my best friend, she's got a little more attitude, a little more teasing. She entranced me and I signed up for her next night, a much longer session. And another, before I realized I was in far too deep. I couldn't disappear, and I didn't want to give her up.

I started watching cam girls when my fiance dumped me. I couldn't imagine getting close to someone else for sex. So I found it, anonymous pleasure. I created a Dominant persona for the website. But it's become part of me. Something I want to explore. Preferably with Cinnamon.

I want more. I need to touch her, taste her, feel her.

How much more do I want from her? I'm not sure. I'm not ready for a romantic relationship.

"You're always working. You need to hang with me more. I'm still lonely after Sherry left." I'm kind of whiny about it, but I miss her.

She put her hand over mine. "I'm sorry. Next weekend, I'll take Saturday night off and we'll hang out."

I lace our fingers together, and my heart skips a beat. Pathetic. Why can't I lean over the table and kiss her? What if I'm in too deep and she's mad I didn't tell her it was me watching her all those nights? That my money paid for all the sex toys and for her to spread her legs.

I wish I had more money to buy all her time. I don't want to miss a minute of her shows, her body.

She looks to the door.

"I'm sorry I'm whining about my life. You have your own problems."

"No, I need to make time for you." She let go of my hand and kissed my cheek. "Next weekend."

Her scent lingers while I take my time finishing my drink. She needs time to get home, change her clothes and do her makeup. She never wears any makeup in life, but on the cam, it's heavy. And hot.

Twenty minutes later I log on. She's not online, so I fix myself a drink and take off my pants.

At three minutes before our scheduled time, she's online. I watched her adjust the camera, then her hair and breasts.

CallMeSir: Hello Cinnamon.

It's a good this is text. I almost called her Chloe. She blows a kiss at the camera. "Hello TJ. What are you doing?"

CallMeSir: I'm good. Had a drink with a friend earlier. Having another one while I talk to you. How are you?

She leans forward so her ample breasts are on display and I get a good look down her shirt. She was covered at the bar. Probably for the best. An erection may have been telling. "I had a drink with my best friend."

CallMeSir: Two hot girls in a bar, if I had been there I would have sent a drink your way.

Misleading. I'm supposed to be getting closer to the truth not further away from it. She smiled. "I'd like that. After I accepted your drink would you come over and chat me up?"

She didn't correct me. Interesting.

I like where the conversation is going. I can use my fantasy of how the evening would have ended, and her fantasy of being picked up. If I merge them, it will arouse me even more.

CallMeSir: I'd come over and give you both a smile, but you'd know from my gaze lingering it was you I want. Are you wearing that outfit at the bar?"

Her eyes bounce to something in front of her then back to the cam. She is looking right in my eyes, as if she can see me. It's like a jolt of electricity. I have enough pent up energy. Maybe this can go quickly so I can get off fast. We can spend the majority of the hour chatting if she wants. But the more I get to know her, the more I realize she's very much like Chloe, despite the bluster of her performance.

I have a thin line where I can only repeat Cinnamon comments to Cinnamon and I can only repeat Chloe things to Chloe. I haven't mixed up their words yet, but I may soon.

Cinnamon suits her so well. Sugar and spice, and everything nice, that's what my Chloe is made of. I can also call her Cin, which fits her on cam persona, too well.

She wants to see me next weekend. I don't know if I can stop from touching her this time.

"Yes, I'm wearing this outfit to the bar."

No way would Chloe wear something that revealing to the bar. Fuck, I want her to. How can I ask her to dress up like my slutty Cinnamon? She's leaning on the desk, waiting for me to answer.

CallMeSir: I'd definitely come over and buy you a drink. If I could get through the crowd surrounding you.

She smiles and leans back, a gleam in her eye. "As soon as I saw you, I'd send my other admirer's away. The sexiest man in the bar, the best smile. Fuck-me-eyes." She groans. She's good at this. Making me feel like I'm the one she wants, the only one in her world.

CallMeSir: What should I bring you to drink? A nice red wine? A girly drink with grenadine and fruit juice?

"Sex on the beach. Leg spreader. Screaming orgasm." With each drink name she raises her eyebrows. I google them quickly. "If you're searching for them, look up the naughty version of the leg spreader."

Equal parts vodka, gin, rum, and tequila. That would probably lower inhibitions.

CallMeSir: I think I'd stick with the screaming orgasm and I don't mean the drink. Partly because it's a promise for later, and part because I like my partner to be sober.

"A promise? Are you confident or cocky, Sir?" Her tone is taunting.

CallMeSir: Confident. There's your bratty side coming out, Little Cinnamon. Pinch your nipple.

She sticks her tongue out but grabs her right breast. Her fingers tweak her nipple through the spandex outfit. The lighting isn't good enough so I can see her nipples tighten with need. I need the outfit to disappear.

CallMeSir: You looking to get punished?

"Usually."

That's true. I laugh. I lean closer to the monitor and feast on her face. She's sexy and charming. I knew Chloe was, but not like this.

CallMeSir: So I buy you a drink and you kick your admirer's out. It's just you and me. We have a few drinks, then I put a slow song on the jukebox and ask you to dance.

"I thought this was a bar, not the club."

CallMeSir: I don't care. I want to feel your body against mine.

"Let's get out of the bar then. Your place or mine?"

CallMeSir: Yours.

We both know what her room looks like. She knows what mine looks like too, but I can't tell her that. I've been in her room. But she's transformed it somehow for the show. There's more textures, different fabrics hanging around the room, hiding her personal effects. Candles are on almost every surface for soft lighting and mood. But she has a video light on her too, it illuminates her face, so I can see every expression.

She snaps her fingers. "We're in my room." She grins, I love that silly grin. "Do you want a glass of wine?"

CallMeSir: We had a few drinks at the bar. I'm more interested in your body against mine.

"I know what I'm wearing. What are you wearing?"

CallMeSir: Jeans and a light blue dress sh--

I pause before I hit send. That's what I was wearing at the bar. I delete the last few words.

CallMeSir: Jeans and a T-shirt.

"What color are your eyes?"

My eyes? I've never thought of it, but what does she imagine I look like. Does she think I'm some guy in his mom's basement? Older, divorced? Unattractive perhaps? Unable to get a date?

CallMeSir: Boring brown.

"Brown isn't boring. Brown is soulful, deep, romantic. They darken during arousal. They lighten during orgasm. Or are you calling my eyes boring?"

CallMeSir: Your eyes? Never. Not one part of you is boring. Can we get the part where I strip your dress off?

"You want me naked do you? Not very gentlemanly."

CallMeSir: I'm not feeling like a gentle man. Get naked, Cinnamon.

She strips her dress off, exposing her nipples, a shade darker than her skin. The entire evening with her at the bar I thought of this moment. It took all my self control not to reach over and cover one of them with my hand, to tease her perfect nipples.

She dances around in front of the camera, showing off her body. She still has her panties on, but I don't comment. It's a good thing she had jeans on at the bar, the temptation to touch her bare thighs may have overcome me. And I wouldn't have stopped under her skirt, I would have made her come before I let her go. Right there in the bar, I would have made her scream.

CallMeSir: You are so fucking gorgeous.

I hit enter. I shouldn't have said that. It's crossing lines, emotional lines.

"Thank you." She slides back into her chair. Her hands cup her breasts and she plays with her nipples. Just how I like to start off our play.

CallMeSir: I bet your skin tastes like honey.

"Mmm." She rolls her nipples between her thumb and finger.

CallMeSir: How has your deep throat practice been going?

"Fine. You want to see?"

I want my dick down her throat.

CallMeSir: Yes, little miss.

She reaches down to the floor and pulls out the dildo. The one I bought her. She wets it with her tongue, while she stares into the camera, right into my eyes.

I drool as she sucks on the end of it. My hand palms my dick through my boxers. I lean back in my chair to watch the show, but she continues teasing me.

CallMeSir: Cinnamon, are you being a bad girl? Suck that fake dick for me.

I want to go back to the bar and instead of letting her go home, I take her into the bathroom or the back alley and push her against the nearest wall and fuck her until we both come. Then take her home and make her come over and over for the rest of the night.

On screen, she pushes the dildo into her mouth. I watch her throat bob as it disappears. She gags a little and pulls it out. "I'm getting good at it TJ."

CallMeSir: You are.

I can't wait until her lips are wrapped around my dick. If she's not too upset it's been me on the other end of the chat screen.

She swallows the dick once more. Mine jumps to attention.

CallMeSir: Rub it against your pussy. Through your panties. I want to see them wet.

She tips the camera so it's on her crotch. I watch, pretending it's my body rubbing against hers. It will be soon. I will make a plan to tell her the truth. But this is too good, too fun. Once she knows, emotions will be involved. I'm not ready to be vulnerable again.

CallMeSir: You were looking for pain earlier. Slap the dildo against your pussy. It had better hurt.

She hits against her, but I can see it's not hard enough to hurt. I can't hear it. My fingers are on the keyboard, but the next slaps come through clearly and she whimpers.

CallMeSir: Good girl.

I never would have guessed Chloe was a masochist. I guess she wouldn't guess I'm a sadist either.

The camera pans back to her face. "Is that good Sir?"

I check the time. We have twelve minutes left. I want her to come more than once.

CallMeSir: Yes, for now. Take off your panties, fuck yourself with it. Make yourself come for me.

I wrap my hand around my dick. She pans the camera back to her nether, so I can see her being spread wide open for my pleasure. She pounds herself with it, her other hand rubbing her clit.

I want to bury my face between her legs. I want to pound into her. I want to make her shake under my touch. Her legs wrapped around me, her moans bouncing off my skin.

I'm tempted to log off and show up at her doorstep and show her real pain and pleasure.

She's shaking already, coming from my instructions, getting off knowing someone is watching.

"Fuck that felt good, TJ. It's been awhile since I had a good orgasm. No one, I swear no one, gets me off like you do. I tell other people that, but with you it's true."

I smile at my screen. She's being sincere, I know her tells. I know her better than she knows herself.

CallMeSir: Good. I like that. I'll be slow to type because I'm jerking off too. Get your vibrator and make yourself come again.

She groans, but she follows the instructions. "You're a sadist."

CallMeSir: You have no idea.

She smiles as her vibrator buzzes to life.

CallMeSir: I want to see your face this time.

The camera stays on her face, the vibrating pleasure device disappears from the screen. I can still hear it, and I know it's on her because her face changes. "Back to the scene. You're here, you get me naked, then what? You push me down on the bed and pound me until you fill me with your cum?" She continues the fantasy we were building.

CallMeSir: No, first I'd spank your ass. Then I'd torture your nipples. Use the clamps and twist them.

I want to jerk off thinking about being inside of her, while I watch her come over and over. But creating the fantasy is a mindgasm, another type of pleasure.

CallMeSir: I'd put you on your hands and knees and pound you until you came on my dick. Then I'd have you lie on your back and I'd lick your pussy until you begged me to stop. Then I'd crawl over you and make love to you, slow and sweet until I couldn't take the teasing, then I'd fill you with my cum.

Her mouth is hanging open. "Fuck," she says softly.

CallMeSir: I'd let you sleep for a few hours, then I'd wake you so you could clean my dick off. I'd fill your mouth, or splatter your breasts. Then I'd put you in the bath, wash you off. Once you were dry, we'd start over again.

Her eyes have rolled back in her head. I imagine she's moving the vibrator around on her clit.

CallMeSir: Is next weekend good for you?

Her eyes widen, but then her shoulders jerk. She's close. I grab my dick and stroke faster. She's coming, her body is shaking. I type as fast as I can with one hand.

CallMeSir: Keep the vibrator on you. Don't stop until I say you can. I haven't come yet and you need to take care of me.

"I can't," she wails.

CallMeSir: You can do it for me Cinnamon. I want you to keep going.

I keep stroking my dick, watching her face. Fuck, she's gorgeous.

I use my typing hand to stroke my balls. She looks distressed but determined. "That's right girl," I say to the screen. "That's my good girl Chloe. You keep that on you until I come. I'm so close, baby."

I push back from the computer so I don't mess up my keyboard. Ah there it is. I feel the peak and my hips jerk as I ejaculate. It spurts several times before relaxing in my hand.

CallMeSir: You can stop.

She shakes her head. "So close," she says.

CallMeSir: One more, Cin.

I watch the screen while I wipe my mess up. She looks tense, but then I see her shaking. It starts with her shoulders, and moves down her body. She moans deeply as it flows through her. And something thumps to the floor, the vibrator I assume.

CallMeSir: Are you okay?

She opens one eye. "Yeah. I'm definitely going to bed. I had a few drinks with friend before this. And I'm done for."

CallMeSir: Thank you Cin.

I add a tip to her account.

CallMeSir: I'll see you next weekend.

"I might not be available Saturday, might be Sunday."

When I was at the bar she promised to see me next weekend. I have to tease her.

CallMeSir: You have a date?

"I'm seeing my best friend. He's still hurting after a break up and I haven't spent much time with him recently."

I love her. Both parts of her, Chloe and Cinnamon. I don't know why she started this, and if she wants to keep doing it, I don't have a problem with it. It's her life. But I can't see her again without touching her, without making her come in person.

I log off and shower before crawling into bed. I open my phone to find a message from Chloe. A selfie of us she took at the bar, making a silly face. She's beautiful and I *need* to let her know.

Night Three: Hard and Fast

Chloe

I open the door and lean against the jamb. My cat, Pussy, rubs against my legs. She knows better than to go further than the doorway but she pokes her head into the hallway. Who can blame her from wanting to get a glimpse of Taylor?

He saunters down the hallway, his form taking up most of the space. It's just his confidence that makes him seem larger than life. But he could qualify to be the definition of tall, dark, and handsome. A sexy smile, dark wavy hair, and soulful eyes. I've looked into those eyes so many times, they no longer make my heart skip a beat. Holding a guy while he cries about his ex cements a friendship in the friendship zone.

"Hello gorgeous," he says, kissing my cheek.

My attention moves to the box in his hands. "What did you bring?"

"Cinnamon buns." He smiles as he holds out the box.

I plaster a smile on my face as my heart plummets. *Holy shit.* This has to be the weirdest coincidence in my entire existence. "Sounds yummy." How can I even speak through my dry mouth? "Should I get plates?"

"Yeah." His eyes hold mine. *Oh god, he knows.*

I rip my eyes from his. *He can't know. There's no way he knows.*

He bends to pet Pussy, singing "What's new Pussycat whoa, whoa," in a sexy baritone. One of his hobbies is playing guitar and singing. He's good enough to join a band, but he refuses. His concerts are for friends only. Live, a capella for me only tonight.

I watch him croon to my cat. *Nope, he knows nothing.* I head for the kitchen. He joins me there as I unwrap the box. What is he going to instruct or quiz me on tonight? Since I don't have a big brother, he's appointed himself my guardian. If I didn't love him so much, this would be annoying.

"I've been craving all things cinnamon lately."

I freeze while reaching for the plates. The word echoes in my head: cinnamon. I sense him behind me and my hands drop to my sides. My heart is beating out of my chest, my insides twisting. His fingers press into my hips, then slowly travel up.

My heart flutters. Taylor? *He knows.* My body goes cold. *How?* "Taylor Jude." I lift my head. "Tay."

He cups my breasts. "Cinnamon." He nuzzles my neck, his lips drag across my hot skin.

"TJ." I relax against him. Questions flood my mind, concerns, anger. How long has he known? The whole time. He saw me. He chose me. He hid it from me.

I want to twist away, but he's sucking on my earlobe and I might melt into the floor. His hands are moving under my shirt. Why didn't I put a bra on? Oh god, he's pinching my nipples. My pussy floods with desire for TJ. Taylor. It's so mixed up in my head.

"I asked if this weekend was good for you. You didn't answer, and I wanted to tease you with the cinnamon buns, but I couldn't keep my hands off you."

"Why didn't you tell me before?" The words are like smoke, I choke on them.

His thumbs soothe my nipples with light circles. I don't care, I want him so bad. I want all those things he promised.

"Remember when you said no one else makes you come the way TJ does? It's the same for me. But each private show, made me want to see you, Chloe. And each time I saw you I wanted to touch and taste you." One hand slides down and cups between my legs. My body grinds against his hand. No doubts in my physical desire for him.

My mind is another story. I close my eyes. Do I want this? Am I going to ask all my questions or give into my desires?

"You're tense. Should I stop?"

I shake my head. "I'm just thinking about if you undress me, you'll see my underwear." My hands flutter against my thighs.

"I've seen your underwear. I've seen all of you. I've dreamt of tasting you." His mouth is close enough so the words brush against my earlobe.

I turn in his arms, facing him for the first time since his confession. His eyes are heated, sexy. Anything but boring brown.

I shake my head. It's settled in my mind, the questions can wait. I want his, TJ's hand on me. Taylor. I look up at him, my heat reflects back at me. "I want you."

"You'll let me be in charge? Be as submissive as you are as Cinnamon?"

"Tonight I am Cinnamon." I stretch and press my lips to his.

He shakes his head. He turns me in his arms. "Call me TJ." Taylor's lips press just behind my ear and travel down my neck. His hands cover my breasts, massaging, teasing my nipples. "I always loved your breasts. After you took your top off it was difficult for me to talk to you without picturing you naked."

"You are such a guy."

"I'm glad you noticed." Fingers squeeze my breast, hard enough to make me cringe, my knees go weak, the pain turns me on more than in chat. He kisses me, for the first time. I spent more time than I'd admit during his broken heart-phase wondering what it would be like to kiss him. And kissing TJ haunted my fantasies. Now it's all coming true.

"Do you like that?" His mouth is against my ear.

Unsure of what to say, it takes me a few seconds to straighten my head. "I didn't know you were dominant."

"I am. So when I undress you, you won't fight me?"

"I'll be good."

Taylor's eyes are intense as he unbuttons my shirt and pulls it away from my body. "Don't move." I remain still while he circles me, his eyes caress my body. "Not my favorite outfit of yours."

"Which is your favorite?"

"Your skin. I guess the red lacy if I have to choose." He stops in front of me. "Bedroom then you get naked."

I follow silently. My skin sticking at the inner thigh as I walk.

"What were the order of events I promised? Spank you, fuck you from behind, let you sleep, show me your deep throat progress, come on your body, wash you off, make love to you."

All the liquid in my body is flowing between my legs. My mouth is dry, too dry to speak. "Yeah."

"The first time has to be hard and fast. I've been fantasizing about this for so fucking long, I won't last once I'm inside you."

I can only stare at him as he pulls my skirt off.

He licks his lips as his eyes caress my skin. "I forgot the part where I bury my head between your legs."

"I think we can skip the sleep part as well for now. You also forgot a spanking." I need him to inflict pain on me.

"Good thing we have the whole weekend."

Just the weekend? My worries are pushed away by his fiery gaze on my skin. My panties are still on, but the rest of me is bare to him. His eyes, his instructions, his touch.

My lungs burn. I forgot how to breathe. I suck in air.

"Don't look so afraid, spice. I promise nothing but pleasure."

I know. But... "Spice?"

Taylor grins then swoops in for a kiss. When he lifts his head, his expression is all business. "Cinnamon - spice. Pleasure." We move to the bed and he lays me back.

He covers me, his clothes scratching my skin. He whispers for me to close my eyes. His mouth slides over my skin, shoulder to belly, my legs part in anticipation. He returns to my breasts: lick, suck, nibble. I've fucked him a dozen times, but it's all been foreplay for tonight. Nothing could have prepared me for TJ in the flesh.

His mouth is so hot down my torso it's like being branded. He lies between my legs and presses a kiss against my pussy so heated my skin blisters with the need for more. An urgency to come floods me, I grip his head. "Please, TJ. Fuck please, I need to come."

Taylor lifts his head with a growl. "Say my name, Chloe. Say my name while you come so it's imprinted on you. No one else can make you come like me, right?"

My fingers brush through his hair. He teases me with light flicks of his tongue across my clit. "Taylor," I moan. "Please, Tay. I need..."

"The more distracted you get the longer this will take."

"Taylor. Taylor Jude Denn. Taylor. Taylor... Taylor... Taylor." His name repeats on my lips as the fireworks of pleasure detonate in my nerves. The shaking feels like it may go on forever, the pleasure echoing endlessly through my body.

My eyes are blurred but I watch him, unable to take my eyes off him for a moment. He undresses and I try to force focus on myself. I stretch my hands toward him, wanting to run my fingertips over his honey-looking skin. I can't reach him before he grabs my wrists. "I'm in charge," he reminds me. "You did good with saying my name."

He pushes my wrists over my head while his mouth captures my bottom lip. I suck on him, inhaling my scent from his mouth, swallowing my desire. "Thank you," I say.

I'm still shaking but he flips me over. "Hands and knees," he urges me. Somehow my limbs stabilize under me and I'm on all fours before him. "Condom," he pants.

"I'm on the pill. If you trust me." I glance back at him. "You said you wanted to fill me with cum." Also, although some guys have a fetish for period blood, it's not my thing, so I control my cycle so I can perform more days.

His cock probes my entrance. His fingers dig into my ass as he pushes inside. I'm shaking, instantly, primed to come. His movements are slow, teasing. I try to submit, to wait, but I want him to pound me.

"You're so impatient, Cin." Taylor massages my butt hard enough to make me whimper. The pain helps me relax, I can sink into it. "Your body is gripping me so sweetly. I want to savor this." Thrust, slow pull out, breath, breath, thrust.

He squeezes my hips and pounds me. I whisper his name.

"Say it louder, Chloe."

"Taylor."

"Who do you belong to Cin?" He pauses.

"You. TJ. Fuck me Taylor."

His fingers bruise my skin as he claims my body. He rams me with a howl as he comes. I collapse, the blankets cushioning my fall. He drags me up to the pillows, my head on his shoulder as he holds me.

"That was way fucking better than my fantasies."

I close my eyes, now that the haze of lust has passed the questions are crowding in.

He kisses the top of my head. "I should have told you when I first found you. But that first live show, you turned me on. And you know how you said no one else makes you come the way I do, I felt the same."

I nod. "Why were you on the site?"

"After Sherry left, I was horny, but I didn't want to get involved with anyone. Porn was way too anonymous."

A chill fills my body. I pull away a little. "So you just want…"

He holds me. "I can't promise anything. I'm still hurting from Sherry." He closes his eyes.

I frown. I almost say 'I love you,' but there are lingering questions. A breath escapes my lungs. "I was on there, because my rent was increased and I couldn't afford where I live."

"Why didn't you tell me? I would have helped."

"That's why. I'm not relying on someone else to pay my rent. This works." It pays so well I'm considering it as a full time job. "Plus the orgasms."

"I don't have a problem with it. I was your client. I'll keep paying you."

No, no no. "I'm not letting you pay me for sex."

"Just for one show a week."

I shake my head. "It's too many lines. Even if you aren't emotionally involved, I am."

He kisses my head. "I am too, how many times have you propped me up when I thought I would die from the pain?"

Enough times. "That's what friends do."

"We are more than friends now." He looks down my body. I'd all but forgotten we were naked.

"So now what?"

"I will get the cinnamon buns, maybe spank you, then cover you in come. Then clean you up." He grins.

I smile back, my heart sinking. That's not what I meant, but it's okay for now. I have to move forward carefully, keeping my heart close. I don't want to give it away to him if he won't commit. Nor will I give up my work. But I will let him give me a few more orgasms this evening.

Night Three: Soft and sweet

T.J.

I know I should leave. Chloe's wants radiate through our conversation. She wants more, a relationship, a commitment. I want those too, but my heart is still bruised. My emotions are tender, they limp instead of skip, dance, or sing.

I should leave, but I can't. I want more of Cinnamon, to see her squirm, hear her moans. To fill her in all the ways we talked about.

I leave the bed and get cinnamon buns. I return to Chloe and open the box. While I sit beside her, I feed her bites of sweet dough and tease her. She nips my fingertips, and I let her suck them clean.

"You're good with your mouth, Cin. Time for you to show me the result of your deep throat practice."

She looks down at my cock. It's half hard. "I don't know if I can take anything that large."

"You have bigger dildos." I stroke my erection to grow it. She reaches for me, but I catch her hand. "On your knees on the floor, proper blow job position."

"There are dozens of ways to give a blow job. There is no right way."

"Sassy Cinnamon. I'll punish your smart mouth later." If we don't pass out from exhaustion. "On the floor."

She grins and slides to the floor. She was pushing for punishment and I'm tempted. I wind my fingers into her hair, gripping her. She wraps her fist around my cock, I remain still while she guides me into her hot mouth. Slide, suck, slide.

"No hands," I command. "Put them behind your back." I glance over and catch our reflection in her closet doors. She has the old style ones that are floor to ceiling mirrors. I can watch myself fucking her mouth and that may be the most erotic act I've experienced.

Her hand drops away and she bobs her head. In and out, my dick slides. "Yes." I lean back a little, letting her pleasure me. She pulls me deeper into her mouth. I want to yank her hair into submission and fuck her.

"Deeper baby. Take me all the way in, swallow me down."

Her moans turn to choking as she takes me to the back of her throat. She holds me there, a couple heartbeats before she sputters my rod out of her lips. My fingers massage her scalp. "Good girl. That's my good girl. Take me back in. Do it again."

Chloe's lips part and she wraps herself around my cock again. She's a fucking angel. She presses right to the back, swallowing the head again. Her mouth holds me one heartbeat longer. And then she sucks, pure pleasure pulsing through my body. Her fingers feather my balls, her nails scratching lightly, perfectly. She's either had practice or she's just naturally good.

Her tongue swirls the head of my cock and my control slips. I tug her hair a little tighter. "You stay still. I'm going to fuck your mouth. When I come I'll cover your breasts. Okay?"

She nods a little. Her eyes are wide. Which part is new for her? I don't care I'm going to come in her mouth shortly.

I pull her hair so tight she must be uncomfortable. She doesn't show it, or maybe it relaxes her, she looks calmer. I thrust into her mouth. I have to be careful not to hit the back of her throat, she already had enough of that today, I don't want to bruise her.

My balls pull up and I pull out of her mouth. I stroke my erection, trying to keep it pointed at her chest until I burst all over her. My cum drips down her skin making her look delicious. My dick is half limp when I pull it from her lips. "I knew you could handle it." I pinch her nipples, my fingers sliding through my cum on her.

"It's sticky, and it was hot. But it's getting cooler."

"You look hot as hell." I want to fuck her again; I just came and I want her again.

"Do you want to continue with the fantasy or call it a night?"

"Are you done?" she asks, getting to her feet. She avoids my gaze.

"I don't want to be done." Ever. "After that, you deserve a reward. Then the bath."

"What sort of reward?" Her worry turns to excitement

"Pain, Cinnamon. You asked for it repeatedly, so now I will hurt you." I sit on the bed. "Over my knee, and I'll spank you."

She can't move fast enough to throw herself over my knee.

Fuck. How'd I get so lucky that I can kiss, spank, and fuck my dream girl? Her ass is beautiful, her soft skin tempting me. "And now to turn your ass my favorite color." I rub her ass with one hand, my mind racing ahead to fucking her again.

Slow down. I force a gulp of clean air. This is Friday night, as long as we have nowhere to go, and she agrees, I can possess her the rest of the weekend. I can brand her. Get her addicted.

And that's where the plan goes wrong. I want to get her addicted, but I might get myself addicted. Accidentally. When she is in top form she's difficult to resist.

Spank her ass red as my favorite pair of her underwear. I grip the muscle harder, digging my fingers into her. She is still so I slap her, hard, she jerks. "Checking if you are awake."

"I'm awake. You make it hard to be good when you tease me."

"That is true." I slap her ass, lightly to start. I should have had her retrieve her paddle before I started. More pain, see if she was spanking as hard as it looked. There is something about skin to skin that's more satisfying. I increase the speed and weight of my hand until she is moaning. The bloom of red grows with each hit. The more she moans the harder my blows become.

I freeze, caressing the rosy cheeks. My rosy cheeks. Tonight they are mine. This weekend she is mine. I hope she doesn't have plans. "You look gorgeous. How does it feel?"

"Lovely. I can take it harder."

"Can you? Maybe you should grab your paddle and we'll see what you can handle. What's your stopping word?"

She rolls off my lap and crosses to her computer desk.

"My safe word is donkey."

"Donkey?"

The box of toys is under the desk. Her body blocks my view so I concentrate on her ass. "Are you trying to get me to bruise you?" I stroke my cock while I wait for her. It wasn't many minutes ago I came, but her jerking on my lap while I spank her has me hard again.

I could order her to her knees to suck me off again. Fill her mouth this time. Not yet. She returns with the paddle. "Here you are, Sir." I take it from her.

"Good girl. Hands and knees on the bed. Or would you prefer bent over the desk?"

She blinks at me, confused by the question. I grab around her waist and kiss her. "Never mind my questions. I'll choose the bed." I grab her hair and yank her in my desired direction.

Once she's in position, back slightly arched so I can get a good angle, I bring the paddle against her. No warning, no pretense, no holding back. "Fuck," she yelps, her body shooting forward. She almost falls onto her face.

"You said you could handle harder. Stay there. We need music." I find my phone in my pants pocket and tune into some hard rock music with a beat the speed I'd like to spank her.

"I've never been bruised before."

"Let's see what it takes to get you to stop me."

She nods, her head dropping. "I'm ready. Green."

The paddle makes a great clap as it hits her. It drowns out the music for a moment each time. Her moans rise above the music. She's hurting, but she's trying to power through it. She's trying to be more stubborn than me. I hit harder, making her swear. Again, she whimpers. Another blow and she whimpers, "Donkey." Her body stiffens. A little louder, "Donkey."

I stop and caress her scarlet skin. She falls onto her front, her body shaking. I gather her in my arms and wrap a blanket around her. "You okay?"

Her eyes are shining. "God yes, that was amazing. The last one hurt so much, I thought I might burst into tears."

"I will run a bath. Clean you up was next. Then maybe let you sleep."

She touches the glossy cum spot on her chest. "I like being painted by you. And you promised to make love to me next in your plan."

"If you aren't too tired. We need to pace ourselves. I was hoping we could play all weekend."

"I have a show tomorrow night."

"You can still do it. I'll find something to do while you sell yourself."

"Do you mind?"

"What you do?" How can I complain? I was purchasing what she was selling. "No."

"Not jealous?"

"No. As long as we hide nothing, no one can be jealous. I can't take any lies." Sherry lied about our relationship.

"Okay, no lies." She opens her mouth, but I kiss her. I don't want to talk. I let my tongue swirl in her mouth, tell her everything she needs to know.

Once she's relaxed, I roll off the bed and pull on my underwear. I run the bath, finding her bath salts in the cupboard and dumping a healthy dose into the water. Once it's full, I return and pick her up. She squeals and wraps her arms around my neck.

"What are you doing?"

"Carrying you. What does it look like? You rarely ask silly questions."

This mollifies her and she relaxes her head on my shoulders. In the bathroom, I put her on her feet and help her into the tub. I retrieve a bowl from the kitchen and pour water over her head. She sighs happily as I massage shampoo into her hair.

I wash her body slowly from neck to feet. When she's clean, she pulls the plug and steps out. I insist on drying her body. She looks satisfied wrapped in an oversized fluffy purple towel. "Do you want to cuddle?" I cup her chin and kiss her softly.

She shakes her head, stretching to linger in the kiss. "I want you to make love to me Taylor. Slow and sweet."

Make love to Chloe. I can do that. I can do soft. "Some sugar to go with the spice?" I don't let her answer, I cover her mouth with mine. I slide my tongue past her lips, exploring her mouth thoroughly. My hands slip under the towel, brushing the back of her thighs, using her ass to pull her against me. She whimpers and wiggles against me. Her ass is tender.

Knowing she's sore makes me surge. The two orgasms so far have taken the edge off my need for her. I can do slow now. I can take my time and tease her properly. I bend my knees so I can rub my cock against her cleft while I continue to make love to her mouth. Nipping her lips, stroking her tongue.

I pull back. We need to get horizontal. I take her hand and pull her to the bedroom. Pussy is on the bed, staring at us. I scratch the soft grey fur behind her ear and she arches into my hand. Always wanting more pets, just like her mistress.

"Puss, off the bed." Chloe pushes her toward the edge of the bed. Pussy moves her fluff to the side, but refuses to vacate.

"She's fine. You like having an audience."

"Not my cat. She'll be traumatized. I lock her out during shows."

"That's why I've never seen her on screen. You should introduce her. You should also get on the bed." I pull the towel away and drop it on the floor.

She sits cross legged on the bed, making me smile.

"Lay down Chloe. Let me see your gorgeous body." I stretch on the empty side, my legs at an odd angle to accommodate the ball of fur. Chloe lies on her side facing me, her cheeks are a little pink. Her hand lies on my chest; her fingers stroking the hair and my nipple.

I lean forward, kissing her again. My fingers curl around her breast, molding her to the shape of me. I almost let her feel the bite of my touch before I remember I promised sugar and silk. I roll her back and dip to suckle her. Her back arcs, demanding more. I circle with my tongue, and she digs into my hair. I can't help myself, I sink my teeth into her flesh until she cries out.

My eyes drag to hers, searching for recrimination for the transgression. There is none, her head is tilted back, her throat exposed. I let my teeth sample that tender expanse, she opens further for me. I treat her other breast the same, tame then harsh.

My erection flexes against her side. Her fingers trace the outline through the cotton.

"Bad girl."

Chloe doesn't look sorry. She gives me a sweet smile, a flutter of eyelashes, and a soft kiss.

I can play that way. I press my palm to her mons, sliding across her labia. She's heeded my plea and stopped shaving herself bare, the new hairs rasp across my skin. I need to taste her spicy sweet desire. Two fingers dip inside, stroking her slickness. I lift her fingers to my lips and suck them with a moan of pleasure. I breathe deeply, savouring the scent of how I arouse her.

I make a second pass of her juicy pussy. This time I press my fingers to her mouth. "I love watching you taste yourself." Her smile parts and her tongue slides between my digits.

She lets her saliva flow over me, reminding me of how she sucked the dildo on camera.

"I remember this moment. On cam." My words are more like a series of groans.

The desire to climb over her and pound into her overwhelms me for a moment. I close my eyes, my finger brushing her clit, until the need passes. I will be inside her again.

I keep the teasing touch on her clit until her hips rock. She wants it hard and fast. "I promised soft." Brush, brush, tap. Mellow, soft, easy.

"You're teasing." Her lips are pressed together, barely opening as her frustration leaks out in puffs of air.

Her legs press together, her hips circle. "I'll have to restrain you, Cin," I warn. I press my knee between hers, stopping her from getting her legs too close together. She relaxes her thighs, letting them drop open.

"Better?"

"Good girl." I reward her with a firmer touch. She sighs with relief. I push two fingers inside her, using my thumb to stroke her clit.

Her hand reaches inside my underwear and strokes my erection. Her fingers twisting off the head.

"Sweet Cin," I whisper against her lips.

"I need you inside me TJ." She kisses me this time, her tongue probing the recesses of my mouth.

I push my underwear off and shift my weight over her. She's so wet, so aroused, so ready, my cock glides into her. I tense my thighs as a reminder to make love to her sweet self. She needs me inside, I need her period, all around me, all the time.

I roll my hips, her luscious body grips mine, milking me. My eyes meet hers, our lips pressed together, and without formulation we move as one. Together and part. Her hand wedges between us, and through the lust I remember she needs clitoral stimulation to orgasm. Imagining her touching herself is hot, and she knows her body better than me. Though I should have enough knowledge, I've watched her masturbate enough times.

Her hand vibrates between our bodies as I thrust faster. It's her quivering legs and the way she milks me that forces my pace to quicken. I can taste the orgasm as she muffles her cries against my mouth. I grab her ass, pulling her against me as I drive for my gratification inside her.

My cock is buried deep in her when I climax. Fuck, my body goes limp, lust for her finally satisfied for the evening. She'll rouse me again by morning, but I can rest for a while.

She pushes at me. "Crushing me," she wheezes.

I roll to the side. "Sorry, darling. You drained me there. It will be a few minutes before I can walk."

"That good?"

"Foreplay has lasted more than two months." She's propped on her elbow, looking down at me.

"That's true. I'm starving since we never ate the cinnamon buns earlier. You want one?"

"Yes, please. Will you feed it to me?"

"Possibly. Are you staying the night?"

I smile. "Yes. I have plans on how to wake you in the morning."

Morning One

Morning One

Chloe

I wake to something banging. *Was that my front door? Did someone break into my house? Did one of my fans track me down?* I sit up and clutch my blanket to my chest.

Ow, fuck. My ass hurts.

Oh right, one of my fans tracked me down. Or rather my best friend stumbled on my cam show and needed to fuck me. It's sort of confusing in the post-orgasm haze. Many, many orgasms.

I flop back to my pillows. TJ is out there in my living room or kitchen. Or something. *Please let him be making coffee.* I roll over and press my head into the pillow he occupied last night. It smells amazing. Like sex and spice and Taylor Jude. TJ. I should have realized.

I have questions. To get answers, I will have to move my sore ass out of this bed. Should I get dressed? Maybe my robe. I don't want to advertise there may be more sex. We need to talk. I shouldn't have asked him to spend the night.

Pussy jumps on the bed and nudges against my hand. I scratch behind her ears and she purrs. "What's new Pussycat? You saw some new things last night."

She remains unphased as she pushes against my side. There's more banging, it sounds like pots and pans this time. Did he buy food to make breakfast? This isn't what I thought when he said he wanted to wake me.

I thought there would be oral sex, handcuffs, or pain. Probably all three. Breakfast wasn't even in my thoughts.

I snuggle back under the covers. *Should I go out there?*

I stretch over and grab my phone. I check my email, my private show schedule is full for the next week. There are several too personal emails, I toss them in the trash.

I throw back the blankets, I should help him. Pussy jumps off the bed and runs to the door. I pad to the door where my robe hangs. Taylor is at the doorway, his body blocking my escape. He surrounds me, my heart skips a beat as my eyes dart up.

I could love him.

Love is dangerous for us. We are friends. I don't want to lose that. His heartbreak is not fresh, but the pieces are only taped together, waiting for time to mend him.

There is also the layer of Cinnamon and TJ. *Does he want Chloe? Or does he want Cinnamon? Is Taylor different from TJ? Or is the domination just something I've never seen.*

He grabs my chin and kisses me. "Back in bed. I'm making you breakfast." He pulls the robe from me, slowly the satin slides through my nerveless fingers, the way he slid in me last night, the way his tongue is sliding in my mouth right now.

My limbs are limp when he breaks the kiss. "I know that. I was coming to help."

His lips twitch into a smirk. "You will come all right. For now you stay here. Get your vibrator and use it, but don't come." He waits for me to retrieve the vibrator and lie on the bed before he turns away.

I flick the switch and moan as it touches my pussy lips as he gets to the door. He turns and winks before he exits the room.

Don't come, I repeat to myself as I rub the vibe against my clit. He better fuck me as soon as he gets in here then. A shiver slithers up my spine, circling my head. Is he hard thinking about me? I'm fucking wet thinking about him, about what he might do, about what he did to me. All those times on chat, all the things we talked about doing.

If he had told me in the bar or somewhere neutral, I would have been embarrassed. Instead telling me, while he groped me, I couldn't be anything other than turned on. It's embarrassing I didn't know. I should have... TJ... Taylor. TJ could be initials for a hundred combinations of names. It only seems obvious now.

My legs tremble and I rip the wand away from my body. It hurts to be close and not come. "Hurry," I call.

"You can't hurry perfection," he replies. "Take a break and cool down."

I flip the switch off and pull the sheet over me, curling on one side. I grab my phone again, there's a message from Joelle, a mutual friend of ours. "Joelle wants to know what I'm doing today."

"Getting fucked until you can't walk and don't know your name," he says, at the door holding a plate.

I type back a message. "Hanging with Tay today?" I say.

"No, if she's bored she'll want to see us. Just say you're working."

"I don't want to lie."

"I'll pay you then it's not a lie."

"You aren't paying me for sex again. Ever." I level my stare at him.

He looks unimpressed. "What do you want first?" he waves his hand over the plate.

I reach for the fork and he pulls back, avoiding my grasping fingers.

"I'm going to feed you." He picks up a piece of bacon and waves it.

I snap my teeth at it, but he doesn't let me grab it.

"Say please and open your mouth. It's your food getting cold while you dick around, not mine."

"Speaking of dick..." I drop my gaze to the region of anatomy.

"You'll have my dick in you again soon enough. You need to eat to keep your strength up or you won't be able to walk when I'm done with you, but not for good reasons."

I shiver at the threat. "Please may I have bacon, Sir?" My voice is saccharine sweet, but I open my mouth and he pushes the salty meat inside. I chew it while watching him. He cuts up the pancake.

"So you went out and bought stuff to make pancakes?"

"No, I went to my apartment, as I needed extra frying pans. You have one. How do you live?"

"I only cook for myself. How many do I need?"

"I'll buy you another, otherwise I won't be able to cook here. You won't be able to cook for me."

"You aren't allowed to buy me gifts anymore unless it's my birthday, Christmas, or goddess help us, our anniversary."

"I'll buy you whatever I want." He gives me an indignant look and presses a piece of pancake to my lips.

I take it into my mouth. The syrup is on my tongue first, but the fluffy dough melts my thoughts. We are silent as he feeds me bites of pancake, bacon, and egg. He watches me to see when my mouth is empty before offering another piece. It's the most intimate experience of my life.

When the plate is empty, he sets it on my side table and rolls me to my back. His body covers mine, his weight balanced on either side, then his mouth comes down on mine. For a moment it overwhelms me and I struggle to breathe or think.

Taylor pulls back from the kiss. "You're tense." He shifts to the bed beside me. "Roll over."

I give him a nervous look, but then roll to my stomach. When he comes into view, he's sitting on the side of the bed removing his clothing.

"Going to spank me?" I ask.

"Maybe later." He straddles my prone body and his fingers press into my shoulder muscles.

My breath hisses between my teeth. I'm far more sore than I knew.

"How bad?" he asks, kneading the muscles. His hands are strong. I wish I'd known he could do this months ago, I would have hit him up for a massage long before this.

"Just shocked me how sore I am."

"Focus on relaxing. No worrying about tomorrow or who's in charge. Focus on breathing, through your nose."

I close my eyes and focus on my breath. His hands warm my muscles and it still hurts but not as bad. It maybe even feels good. He moves down my back, stopping when I tense a little, reminding me to breathe. My lower back, my hips, my ass, then down my legs.

Taylor stops at my feet and puts his hands on my ankles. "Now that you are relaxed, let's get more intimate." He pulls my legs apart and kneels between them. His hands grip my inner thighs and dig in until I writhe. "I love watching you squirm."

He kisses my lower back upward to my neck. His mouth sucks my shoulder, and his teeth clenching my muscle makes me squeal. The stubble on his face scratches my neck and cheek as he nuzzles me.

"Do you want to be fucked, Cinnamon?"

"Yes." The word is little more than a breath.

His hand comes down on my ass.

I stretch my neck. "Yes Sir. Please, fuck me Sir."

"Good girl." Taylor kisses me once more on the cheek. He stretches across the bed and I don't know what he's doing until he presses my vibrator into my hand. "For later." He probes between my legs, scratching the stubble, then two fingers stretch my pussy, sliding against my slick inner walls. "I love how wet you get when I touch you."

His fingers withdraw. I whimper at the loss.

"So impatient," he murmurs. He squeczes my ass, the head of his cock presses against my opening.

"Taylor." I arch my back trying to motivate him into filling me.

"Chloe." He pinches my side, but I know he wants this too when he surges inside of me.

"Yes." I relax down again. "You feel so fucking good inside me."

"Turn the vibrator on and put it on your clit but don't come until I tell you."

"You want to torment me."

"Always, baby girl."

I sigh, but it's for show. I love the games he plays. The vibration against my belly makes me gigglc as I push it down between my thighs. I moan as it hits my clit.

"Don't come," he reminds me, before he slides his cock inside me.

Right. Don't come.

"Focus on your breathing, it will make it easier."

I close my eyes again as his thrusts quicken. My body tightens, a wave of pleasure slithers through my thighs. *Oh god, oh god, oh god. How will I not come like this?*

"Focus on your breathing." His fingers dig into my hips, pulling me back to him in mind and body. I hope he presses hard enough to bruise me.

I force my focus to my breathing, slowing it to a count of four. The focus off my pussy helps to slow my descent into bliss but the effect only lasts a short time. The buzz on my clit intensifies as he grips me harder, fucks me faster. My moans match his movements. "Please," I say between gulps of air, "I need to come, TJ."

"Not yet, Cin. Do you need to move the vibe off?"

"Maybe."

"You can take a little more for me."

For him, sure. I think. I open my eyes and focus on the artwork on my wall. A few more thrusts and my need to come reaches fever pitch, I arch my hips away from the vibrator.

"Come for me, Chloe. Squeeze my cock and make me come."

Taylor reaches around and presses the vibe into me, halting his thrusts until I'm quaking. I let a out guttural sound as my body is racked by agonizing ecstasy. He grabs my hips, driving into me, shaking me deeper until he overflows with rapture. I feel his legs quiver against mine.

He collapses next to me, half on me. I smile, unable to move, my gasps turning to panting.

"Fuck." I don't know who mutters that, it's echoing in my head.

He turns his head, so he's facing me. "It's never been this good."

"Sex?"

"Not just sex. When I fed you, my heart was beating out of my chest. Like it was in your chest."

"Yeah. That was intense. Everything has been intense since..." Since when? The computer, I suppose. "Since TJ messaged me. Did you know it was me?"

"I knew it was you. I thought I'd have a laugh, maybe even tell you it was me. You were so fucking hot, Chlo, I couldn't stay away. And then it got hotter and I could barely keep myself from touching you. Every minute I was with you I would fantasize how you taste or feel. It was out of control and last night I couldn't take it one more day."

I kiss him with my heart in my throat. I have many conflicting thoughts. Glad is the dominant feeling. The sex is amazing. Taylor is amazing, I've always known that. But the doubts in my mind need to be addressed. Maybe not today or this weekend, but before I fall in love.

Lazy Afternoon

Sunday evening, I hold Chloe while she rests. I need to return her to my condo, to envelop her by a delicate warm cover and keep her cheerful and took care of and tired from the delight of climaxes. Watching her self-destruct from my fingers or lips or dick is my new most loved distraction.

This weekend has been a vivid class in her body. Ive diligently noticed what my touch means for her. The manner in which she murmurs when I skim her lower back; the manner in which she snorts when I brush her clit daintily; the manner in which she groans when I squeeze her areolas. Thus substantially more with regards to her pleasure focuses and what she disdains.

Be that as it may, adoring her is pretty much as normal as relaxing. Ive cherished her from the beginning. I really want her like I really want daylight and downpour and shading. She improves everything and more splendid. Before this end of the week I never remembered it. On the off chance that I hadnt staggered on her as Cinnamon would I have figured it out?

I need to drink her kisses like water, to devour her words like treats, to go to her voice like a show for my beloved band. Shes everything in my reality and its like riding the rollercoaster of Cloud Nine right to joy.

Sherry who?

I shut my eyes and attempt to rest, however my heart races close by my considerations. Where are we going? Shes never been one to be defenseless or delicate. She secures her heart and brain with a tigers mouth, cautioning snarls if anybody makes abrupt developments, and Ive seen teeth marks from the individuals who got excessively close.

Tigers are just enormous felines be that as it may, and powerless to tummy rubs and scratches behind the ears as some other creature. Our companionship might have let me closer than any other person. Presently I need to stay careful and look as innocuous as a cat until she entrusts me with her fantasies.

I understand that large number of evenings I was crying in her arms, she infrequently discussed herself. I love her, however Im not certain I know her. Ive enlightened her concerning my folks, hitched for 35 years. I expect she has guardians, however no substantial subtleties. Weve discussed our school days, she referenced exiting after her first year. The way to expressions major was cleared with high understudy loans and hardly any work possibilities, so she changed to figuring out how to run an office, which was less exciting yet had a dependable work toward the end. Be that as it may, shes never shared her fantasies. Does she fantasy about running her organization? Or on the other hand would she rather settle down and get hitched, bring up youngsters behind a white picket fence, while exchanging plans with the neighbors and running the PTA?

Maybe the absence of subtleties is only her mindful nature and those evenings being self centered. I will fix that before very long. I will charm her brain as I have done her body. Realize what she prefers, what her identity is, and what she dreams. I will investigate what she needs for the future and find on the off chance that we can assemble it like the third little pig, cooperating, one step at a time.

Shes so wonderful laying alongside me. Her hair spread across the cushion, her lashes laying on her delicate skin.

I kiss her cheek and she blends, her hand coming up to drive me away. I discover her getting a handle on fingers and rub my lips over her knuckles. She moans and settles once more.

I need to awaken her with my mouth between her legs, however she should get sore and I dont need her to think I just need her body. I need every last bit of her, mind, body, soul. I need to adore her, know her, screw her.

She cuddles nearer to me and I shut my eyes. I lay my hand on her watching the ascent and fall of her stomach as she tracks down break from her concerns and my actual requests. Is it true that she is stressed? What happens in her mind? Rather than one more round of musings I match my breathing to her example and float off.

At the point when I wake, its loaded up with extreme delight. Fuck, her mouth is folded over my dick, currently hard.

I settle my hand on the rear of her head and scratch her scalp. She lifts her head. I trust this is OK.

Alright? Being woke with a sensual caress is past alright. I hack to make a sound as if to speak as she takes a gander at me tensely. Its beautiful screwing extraordinary. I twist my fingers into her hair.

She twists to her deliberate undertaking: mouth screwing my dick. My body gets more tight inside, hustling for climax, in spite of having so damn numerous with her. I utilize my hold on her hair to pull her away.

Since Friday night, I have screwed all her ways I can imagine and a couple of I hadnt considered. Weve snuggled, stared at the TV, ate Chinese food, and she did a cam show while I went to my loft to shower and change clothing.

This is our last couple of hours in our air pocket. She will need to talk and I dont have replies.

I dont need to climax alone. I need you accompanying me. I pull her hair until she stops.

She tosses one leg over me and rides my lap. With two hands she strokes my cockerel.

Cinnamon, if it's not too much trouble, child.

She smiles at me.

Chloe. I'm frantic for her. She could break me. In any case, she takes me inside, she moves around me. Like a dream, similar to my fantasies, similar to heaven.

A humming makes my consideration falter. It comes from her body and murmurs through mine. After a second, I understand its a vibrator she squeezed between her legs.

She curves her back as she screws me, taking us higher. Im going to come, she sings.

My body grasps. Im not too far off with you, holy messenger.

Her feet jerk, her thighs shudder, her arms shake. Shes lost in her pleasure, her groans repeating, however she moves constantly. I hold her hips, banging into her until our joy merges like our bodies, becoming one snapshot of flawlessness.

I sit up and kiss her, fold my arms over her, and pull her down with me. I support her against me.

That was the best wake up Ive at any point had, I murmur. I need to leave. I need to end on a high note and nothing will be superior to this second.

Each air pocket needs to explode. She pulls back and there are tears in her eyes. I kiss her cheeks and hold her while she cries. When shes done I clean up and wash away her tears.

We dress unobtrusively. Gives up out, track down something to eat, and play vacationer, I say. I cannot remain in this loft realizing this day will end and I need to get back to the real world. My condo, work tomorrow, the remainder of our lives.

I need to say I love you, however its insufficient to portray how I feel.

Much thanks to you, she says, kissing my cheek.

For what?

For not posing inquiries.

With regards to her tears. There were no inquiries to pose, I feel something very similar. I support her head and kiss her delicately. There was nothing to inquire.

I grasp her hand and we stroll outside together.After several hours, I park at her loft. I kiss her once more. Sick see you during your show.

She goes to me. No. We cannot do that any longer. You cannot pay me for my shows. We are involved. Im not taking cash for sex from my beau. She tips her jaw up.

Then, at that point, imagine its not me. I dont figure your pay ought to experience since I incidentally tracked down your show. I recline.

Not occurring, Taylor. That is not how our relationship will function.

She sets her mouth in a firm line, arms got over her chest. She doesnt say it yet her eyes say screw you.

I put my hands up. Set aside some effort to think about it.

She watches out at the structure for the flicker of my eye, then, at that point, back at me.. Alright, considered. Would you be able to consent to my terms? Im not a screwing noble cause case. I dont need you to deal with me. Alright?

I open my mouth, then, at that point, close it.

She pushes her entryway open. Set aside some effort to think about it.

Before I can reply, she escapes the vehicle. I ponder following her, however shes excessively resentful. Following will want to push and shell explode. Which is all well and good. She really wants space.

I watch until shes inside then commute home. I send her a goodnight message and she reacts with something very similar.

The air pocket didnt recently burst. It detonated in my face.

A Night Out With Friends

On Monday evening, I give my companion Joelle some espresso. She grins at me as I sit down opposite her in my loft. I want counsel. I rub my sweat-soaked palms against the well used texture of the rocker I took from my folks when I moved out.

I realized something is up when you called me at lunch.

Joelle is companions with Taylor. We have one of those clich companion gatherings. I knew Joelle and Travis from school, Travis worked with Taylor who was dating Sherry. What's more, we continued to run into one another until we were a gathering. We used to have others, however we sort of cemented as five when Sherry left and we fortified around Taylors misfortune. The entirety of our misfortune. She was our closest companion. She left us all.

I take a full breath. Alright. I need to let you know a few
things. Try not to pass judgment on me.

I recount her the account of my lease and my subsequent
work and Taylor.

Youre screwing Taylor? Joelles espresso sloshes over the
edge of her cup. She pushes her finger in her mouth.

My eyes roll up. Indeed.

It bodes well. You were close with him after the separation.

We were. That was the part that didnt bode well, truth be
told it was the specific inverse to me. Before he knew me as
Cinnamon, we were dearest companions, however just
companions. He was attractive, yet it was absolutely
impossible that he saw me more than the young lady whose
shoulder he cried on for quite a long time. I had a keen
interest in him since the time we met. Who wouldnt need
Taylor? He is stunning.

I don't know.

Youre both ravishing.

Taylor is. Im me. Thick gut, wild hair that is neither brown nor blonde, and a nose that is too large.

Youre wonderful, Chloe. You have certainty that most ladies dont have.

I shrug and recline in my seat, taste my espresso.

So whats the issue? You need a responsibility and hes not prepared? Or then again he needs you to stop your cam work?

He needs to keep paying me for hidden shows. I dont need my sweetheart paying me for sex. That is an excessive number of lines crossed.

Joelle gestures. Alright.

I dont need to depend on him like that. He said I dont need
your pay to endure on the grounds that I coincidentally
tracked down you. Like I cannot find another person who
will pay me.

I let you know how hot you are.

Im on a tirade now. Cash changes things. In the event that
you have the cash, you have the power. I dont need to
depend on anybody for cash.

So youll never get hitched to somebody who gets more
cash-flow than you?

Sick consistently have my own wellspring of cash. I watched
my auntie and my sister get swindled in separate by their
spouses who brought in the cash. Neither of them worked,
they had children youthful. Not doing it.

My hands are shaking. I was in school when my sister
separated from her better half. I was three months from my
secretary confirmation a similar preparing my sister had.
Just my sister got hitched around a half year into her first
post-confirmation work, and when she got pregnant a
couple months after the fact, she quit working. Her better
half had a steady employment. She didnt need more.

At the point when you put it that way, Im rethinking my
arrangement to be a strikingly attractive spouse. Joelle
gazes into her mug. Her words could be a joke, however
shes genuine.

You wouldnt be an arm candy spouse, you love your work.

I do however I thought when I wedded and had children, Id
remain at home. She looks distressing and I change from
requiring solace to guidance provider.

Save however much you can now. Simply have a back up
arrangement. Work low maintenance or something like
that.

Holy cow, I never considered it. She drinks from her mug.

I apologize for blasting your air pocket.

Perhaps you saved me from a lot of hurt. How is your sister now?

Care is a battle, her child resembled two when they split. In any case, shes working once more, remarried, has one more child with fellow number two. He has one from another relationship. I wave my hand. Its way more convoluted than my life.

Point of view, hello?

I sit up straighter. Things being what they are, Im not off-base?

No, you are not yet does he have some familiarity with about your sister?

I didnt even make the association until a moment prior. No. He doesnt. Do you think damnation quit attempting to white knight me in the event that I do?

Taylor? Possibly. Im as near him as you and he are.

Our eyes snap together like Lego. Truly? I raise my eyebrow.

She holds her hands up. OK not so close. However close as you and I may be. You figure Trav and Cam would need to watch if they knew your skeleton in the closet?

I wrinkle my nose. Ew, I cannot envision them or any other person I know watching.

Be that as it may, you like Taylor watching.

I didnt realize it was him until Friday. Its Taylor however, if you let me know you didnt have a keen interest in him Id be shocked.

Taylor? So not my sort. Hes got the entire toady vibe. I really want an awful kid, bike, calfskin coat, long hair, tattoos. More than never late for anything. That is all you Chloe. Do you utilize Chloe on the site?

No. My cam name is Cinnamon.

Cinnamon. It suits you to such an extent. She grins over the edge of her mug. You and Taylor have a terrible streak Id never have speculated. Its like discovering your folks had a mysterious radical past. Both of you are the mother and father of our gathering. In any event, when Sherry was near.

Sherry, we seldom talk about Sherry, shes like she who will not be named. Now and again somebody will recount to a story that includes her and when it gets to the part her name comes up, they either skip it or simply change the subject. Its an unwritten principle. In any event in case Taylor is near. He was so crushed after she left. Difficult to fault him since they were months from marriage. Nobody knows why she left. On the off chance that she gave Taylor an explanation he never discussed it.

HIs aggravation is my aggravation.

Im sorry, that is agonizing for you. Quite recently.

I feel so awful for him, you know. They were going to be hitched.

I mean since you were so close with her.

Sherry was my dearest companion. Taylor and I made up for that shortfall for one another. Never saw that.

I know Im not an extraordinary trade for her, but rather I trust Im doing approve as a companion.

I toss a grin at her. You are incredible. Sherry resembled my elder sibling, more established, certain. Dont supplant her, simply be you. Ive known you way longer, at any rate. The occasions you held my hair while I vomited in some fraternity house. Much obliged to you for never letting me be. That qualifies you for dearest companion status.

We did it for one another. Were fortunate the poo we did that we never caused problems. Happy occasions.

A great deal of fun occasions. I love you Jo. We want to hang out additional.

Provided that you can fit me in the middle of your two positions and presently your sweetheart.

Sick figure out time, Jo. Enlighten me concerning your life. Occupy me.

I had espresso with Joelle on Monday evening, Tuesday I had a couple private shows, and Wednesday I didn't have anything. I intended to call Taylor so I could clarify my response, trust damnation comprehend and be more pleasing. Travis messaged me before I wrapped up creating the ideal message. Cam got an advancement and there will be celebratory beverages at our beloved bar.

I arrive five minutes before the delegated time. As I arrive at the entryway, I hear my name. I turn and theres Taylor. Joelles words reverberation in my mind. Continuously on time Taylor. We are indistinguishable, we are the mother and father of the gathering.

I pause and turn. He eases back to a walk when my arms get over my chest. I incline toward the structure attempting to look easygoing as I watch him approach. My heart does an acrobatic daily schedule, awkward like I was as a youngster attempting to sort out some way to resemble the young ladies in the Olympic group.

My inner parts hurt with need to connect, contact him, believe him, inhale him. I need everything Taylor. I need to give myself wholeheartedly to him and apologize for my cumbersome treatment of our disparities. For what reason do I feel so emphatically for him? Its Taylor, weve known one another for quite a long time and I never required him..

All things being equal, I grin while I burrow at the walkway with the toe of my boot. Hi, I say. I dont exclaim I love you or Im sorry or I messed up or even we really want to talk. Sick get to that later.

He kisses my cheek. Hi wonderful. How are you? He grasps my hand.

I need to pull away, uncertain where we stand. Im alright. You?

Fine. The same old thing.

We never discussed the uh, bunch. I point behind with my thumb. Is it true that we are telling them?

Do you figure we can conceal it? His thumb rubs across my palm. How does that vibe so freaking great? Since its Taylor.

I envision twisting my hand away. I dont need to share our relationship, yet I cannot pull back. His eyes meet mine. I told Joelle. I really wanted somebody to converse with and she assisted me with sorting out things. We want to talk.

That sounds terrible. He pulls back, his fingers getting away from my palm.

I bounce forward. No. I really want to clarify. No statements of regret. I wont apologize for my sentiments and requirements. Theres a set of experiences.

He gestures. OK. We can talk. Tomorrow evening possibly?

I have a show. Friday?

Work drinks. You could be my in addition to one and we can leave right on time as could be expected?

His date out in the open? Its work yet. Yahoo. I gesture tranquilly. Sure. Sick

Travis and his date, Lani, do their best not to look like they want to be alone. Their eyes are obviously for each other. She's nice, so maybe we'll be a group of six again.

Taylor sits at the end of the table, around the corner from me. And he won't stop looking at me. I don't know if anyone else notices because I can't stop looking at him either.

He can't stop touching me either, casual touches as we talk.
His fingers brush the back of my hand, or he pats my arm
as he talks to me. I want him. Now.

I excuse myself and from the back of the bar I text him to
get back here. I stay hidden behind a group of people until I
see him. He's looking around from me and I glance at the
table. Travis is looking at Taylor until Joelle distracts him
with a question. I grab Taylor's arm. "Hey, what's-"

I shake my head to cut him off. I pull him down the hallway
into the bathroom and lock the door. Inside the bathroom, I
check the stalls just in case, my hand still holding his.

"Chloe what's going on?"

I run my hand through his hair and plaster my body against
his. "This." I kiss him, my tongue sloppy in his mouth. I'm
buzzed and my inhibitions dropped just enough to make
this seem like a good idea.

Taylor puts his hands on my shoulders, holding me steady.
"I was hoping to take you home tonight."

I shake my head and kiss him again. He doesn't kiss me
back. I take his hand and cover my breast with it. He takes
the hint and kisses me back finally. He teases my nipple
through my outfit. His mouth moves hot on my neck,
sucking, licking, nipping.

"I couldn't go another minute with you looking at me,
touching me but not touching where I wanted."

His hands gather my skirt and pull it up around my waist. One hand presses between my legs, dragging over the lace of my panties. "I meant to keep my hands off you. I'm worse than Travis. Pretty sure everyone at that table knows we are fucking. I couldn't stop myself. I'd pull my hand away and you'd look at me and I was lost."

"You're slow TJ. I was lost when we met outside the bar." I stretch on my toes and kiss him again, shoving my tongue into his mouth, tying his in knots. My hand wraps around his cock through his pants.

He peels our mouths apart. "We can make an excuse and leave."

I undo his belt. "Or you can fuck me here." I open his pants and slide my hand inside. "I'll drop to my knees and suck you off."

"Not in a public bathroom." But he slides his fingers under the crotch of my panties, across my slick lips, and inside, stroking my desire.

He pulls out and paints my lips with it. My tongue darts out and flicks against his digits. He finger fucks me again then feeds me my desire. He licks it from the inside of my mouth.

"Slutty Cinnamon, getting off on herself." When he dips into my panties this time, it's teasing my clit. He knows exactly the right spot, how much pressure to apply, and the rhythm of my body. With the crook of his finger he can bring me to my knees, make me moan. God damn, I grip his shoulders, he can make me come. He covers my mouth to smother my wail of bliss.

"Fuck, Taylor, you're good. But I haven't had an orgasm since Sunday either, so maybe I'm an easy conquest."

"You had private shows last night."

"I faked everything. Even had to fantasize about you to get wet." While I talk my hands work on his pants, freeing his cock. "I think if I sit on the sink I'll be the right height." I work my panties off my legs while looking up at him.

He walks me backwards to the wall and lifts me up. He wraps my legs around my waist as he slides home. "Squeeze me with your legs a little and lean against the wall."

I do as he instructs and the thrusts against me. This was more than I hoped for, but he's fucking me. I've had sex before, I've had casual sex and committed relationship sex. I haven't had a boyfriend in the past eight months, and the last four months have been sexless. I've had good sex; I've had kinky sex; I've had bad sex; I've had indifferent sex.

Sex with Taylor differs from anything I've done with anyone. He knows me, he gets me, he loves me. And I love him. I want to shout it out, but he's kissing me. He halts and stares at me, there's a glint in his eye. I lower my feet to the floor, not daring to breathe.

"Go to the sink, put your hands on the counter, and look in the mirror." Dominant Taylor, TJ, CallMeSir is here.

I cross the room and lean against the sink. The air in this room is cooler than my body and it seems to caress my exposed skin.

He stands behind me and grabs my hair. "Look in the mirror and tell me what you see."

I look at myself, but not myself. My lipstick is smudged, my lips are bruised, and my cheeks are scratched from his stubble. He pushes me down a little, so my back is arched, I can look down my shirt. "I see Cinnamon."

"Cinnamon. The slut, the one who sells herself. The one who wants a quick fuck in the bathroom at the bar."

I say nothing, I stare myself in the mirror. When I don't answer, he tightens the grip on my hair. "Say it Chloe. Tell me you're a slut." His voice is tight, demanding. Not my sweet Taylor, but my Dominant.

"I'm a slut."

"Whose slut?" Her jerks my head.

"Yours."

He rubs his cock against my flooded pussy. "Being called a slut makes you soaked does it?"

"Yes Sir."

He shoves into me, I tense my arms in time to keep from hitting the edge of the counter. He grabs my shirt and pulls it down, then he pulls my breasts free of my bra.

"You like being a slut, so I'll treat you like a slut. If it wasn't our friends out there, I'd walk you through the bar with your skirt around your waist, your soaked panties on display. Let the first guy who offers to buy me a drink a quick grope of you. Something for his spank bank." Taylor's fingers pinch my nipples as he thrusts slowly. "Or maybe he already pays to watch you be a slut."

"Oh god." I arch my back, thrusting against him.

"Not God. Just the guy who owns you. You like being owned, don't you?"

I nod. Our eyes meet in the mirror and his are hard. Verbal answer required. "Yes, I like being owned by you."

He grabs my hips and fucks me. It arouses me, but I can't quite get there. He can sense it, and presses his finger to my clit, circling the nub until we are both shaking.

Someone knocks on the door and I hurry to dress. He doesn't move any faster. We return to the table, amid stares. No one says anything, and I shrug at Joelle's wide eyes. I'll explain later.

An hour later, the party breaks up. I pull out my phone to call a cab, but Taylor's hand is on my arm. He shakes his head. "I'll give you a ride home."

"A ride and nothing else. We'll talk Friday night. Or Saturday morning."

"Don't you recall I own you. You'll do whatever I want," he hisses in my ear. He grabs my arm and propels me out the door and around the corner to his car. He pushes me against the side and kisses me hard. I'm not sure if this is Dominance or anger? Or if there is a difference. It's all too new and too fast. I want to demand pause, but Cinnamon is enjoying it way too much. She wants to be owned. She wants him to demand sex then spread her legs.

He parks at my apartment and pulls me into a bruising kiss. "I want to explain."

"Not tonight. Tonight you are Cinnamon and I am TJ and tonight I own your slutty ass." He squeezes my thigh hard enough so I wince. "Chloe and Taylor will talk later and you can explain your disrespect then. Until then." His fingers tighten until I'm certain there will be bruises I will cherish.

"Of course, Sir. What do you want then?"

He pulls out his wallet and looks inside. He pulls out a couple of bills, twenties and drops them in my lap. "I want you to accept that and I want a private cam show tomorrow after your weekly chat. I'll be on video this time, I'll instruct you. And I'll pay."

I want to argue. Cinnamon nods. "Okay, one night only. And Friday night I will explain my position on our money and our relationship. Or Saturday morning depending how late we are out."

"We'll sleep at my apartment," he decides.

"I need to come home early Saturday to check on Pussy."

"We'll check on Pussy. Both of them." He kisses me softly, but his hand rubs between my legs. I stiffen a little, he will get me going again and I'll have to take care of it myself, which isn't nearly as satisfying as when he fucks me.

He opens his door and comes around to open mine. He puts his hand on the small of my back and walks me to my apartment. We kiss for a moment, then he brushes my cheek. "I'll see you on the show tomorrow and then you'll give me my private show to make up for not talking to me for a couple of days."

"I said yes." Making me agree repeatedly is provoking my anger. I said yes, and I don't want to keep saying it. It's making me question my choices. I kiss him, uncertain of my decision. I shove open the door to my apartment.

He leans against the far wall until I close the door. I watch him through the peephole as he walks away, back down the hall and back to his apartment.

I need a shower and to drink water to counteract the dehydration effect of the alcohol. I didn't get drunk, just buzzed enough to fuck TJ in a bathroom. My phone beeps as I head for my bedroom.

Joelle is sending messages, demanding to know where we disappeared to.

Joelle: *EVERYONE KNOWS*

Chloe: *I know, but I couldn't keep from touching him one more minute. Plus, sex in a public place is really hot.*

Joelle: *How hot?*

Chloe: *I did not tell you this Monday, but Taylor is Dominant. He likes ordering me around, hurting me.*

Joelle: *Does he have a pain room?*

Chloe: *No, just his bedroom. It's not like a romance book. It's Taylor. He called me a slut and fucked me against the wall.*

Joelle: *That sounds hot. Okay, well the guys know and I pretended I had no idea, but I don't think they bought it, so congrats. I think Cam was seriously jealous. It barely made Travis look up, I think he was jealous he couldn't fuck Lani in the bathroom.*

Chloe: *Yeah well. I need to have a shower.*

Joelle: *Call me tomorrow.*

Chloe: *I have work after work.*

Joelle: *Will you tell me where your show is so I can watch?*

Chloe: *No. Good night Jo.*

She sent a pouty face emoji and said Good night. If I thought she wanted to watch, I would send her the link, but I don't think she wants to watch. She wants to tease me.

I grabbed my waterproof vibrator and took it with me to the shower, so I could get off once more. Twice with Taylor was good, but the Domination in the car aroused me again.

Show time

Thursday night, show night. A public show. I dress in my new lingerie I picked up on the way home from work. In the bathroom, I apply eyeliner with a shaky hand. Mascara isn't as tricky, the red lipstick matches my outfit, a lacy merrywidow hooked up to red stocking with matching lace panties.

My mind is distracted from the makeup, leaned against the sink I remember Taylor fucking me in the bar bathroom. I have to check because my memory of him calling me slut is so clear I could swear he's in the room.

My thighs are sticking together as I return to my bedroom. I log on and test my cam and mic.

My show is crap because I watch the clock the whole time waiting for my private show with TJ. My regulars lap it up anyway. I end it early, saying I have a headache.

I am on the edge of my chair, my box of toys beside me, while I wait for TJ to log on.

There's a knock on my door. I grab my phone and send Taylor a message.

Chloe: That better not be you."

Taylor: I have a key, but I'd prefer not to use it."

Chloe: You aren't paying me for sex."

The front door opens. I go to the bedroom door and consider locking myself away from him. Might as well face the inevitable argument. I open it and Pussy rushes in to rub herself around my feet. Poor neglected kitten, I scratch her head.

"I'm not paying you for sex."

His voice makes me jump, but I lift my head slowly. He stands on the other side of the bedroom door, looking sexier than he has a right to be when I'm mad. His hands go up, showing he won't touch me. Why is he here?

I back up and he follows until I'm against my bed. "This will be a private show but only a show. I will not touch you."

"But..." My eyes dart frantically around the room as I realize his meaning. I straighten my back and shoulders and meet his inflamed gaze. He smiles and reaches for me, but then catches himself.

"I bought some new toys for you Cinnamon." He pulls a backpack from his shoulder and pats it.

I want to argue he's not supposed to be buying me things, but they aren't returnable. I sit on the edge of the bed, then jump back to my feet. "Can I sit, Sir?"

"Yes spice. I like the outfit. Red, my favorite color."

"Did you watch my public show?"

"The start of it. You seemed distracted."

"I was. I had an interesting night last night."

"Are you going to share your private life?"

"It wasn't a private moment, at least four people knew we were fucking in that bathroom."

"Dirty slut." He lifts his head from the bag. "If I could touch you, I would lick the skin showing between the slits of your top."

I look down at my outfit. A ribbon holds the lace panels together, they crisscross down my abdomen. He knows how to spark my fire, my eyes flick up.

He holds out something dark and metal. I frown as I reach out and take them. "What is it?"

"Clover clamp. I think you need an upgrade in the torture. If there is weight added to the rings they tighten. We'll add weight later if you can handle it without."

"Should I attach them now?"

"Yes." I expose my right breast first and open the clamps. I bite my bottom lip as the clamp closes on my nipple. I whimper and squirm and Taylor watches me, his eyes growing more intense.

"Safe word?" he asks.

I shake my head, to prove the point I slip the second side on. It hurts to the core and my panties are not made to deal with the flood coming out of my pussy.

"Do you like it?"

I nod as my body absorbs the shock of pain. I can't imagine if they were tighter, but it is more delicious than the typical alligator clamps in my box. "It's very arousing."

"Good to know. Keep your panties on, I want to see them so wet I can see through them."

"I don't think they need to be wet to be transparent." My legs spread and I rub my hand along the slit to soak my desire into the thin fabric. I pull it so it's stretched over my lips, everything but exposed.

"I can smell it. Slide your fingers underneath, get your fingers wet, suck them off. Slowly Cinnamon."

I don't need to thrust inside to get wet my fingers. The ache in my nipples is making me a river of desire. My hand is shaking when I lift it to my mouth. I pull my fingers inside and use my tongue to clean them off.

A moan escapes my chest, deep and primal. I want his mouth on my cunt. I want him to fuck me. Any touch from him would be gratifying.

I lick my lips. HIs eyes on me is more than I can handle, my body shudders. Fuck, I'm coming. I grip the edge of the bed as it overtakes my body. It passes quickly, but leaves me limp.

"DId you come?"

"Yes, Sir. I couldn't help it. You staring at me and the pain and my scent, it was too much."

He doesn't react. "Take off your panties, Chl—Cin."

I unsnap my garters from the stockings. I contemplate his reaction as I hook my thumbs in the sides of my panties and pull them down, careful not to let them catch the stockings on their way to my ankles. The sway of the clamps makes me wince.

He's watching eagerly, his mouth slightly open, his breath falling out. He's back is against the wall beside my closet, his stance wide as he leans on the wall, digging in for the long haul.

"All those men on their computers watching you. They don't know it's an imitation, a facsimile. They don't realize what they are missing. We all want to own a piece of you, but through the screen it lacks the heart and soul.”

I suck in a lungful of air. I’d speak but my mouth is parched, his words depleted any capacity to respond.

“In person, there’s so much spirit and energy. You are brazen and raw sensuality. I want to tame you, own you. I can dominate you, but I can never possess you. Fuck if I don’t want to.”

He pushes away from the wall and I am certain for a moment he’ll grab me, kiss me, fuck me. Instead he moves to the computer chair. He picks up my toy box from the floor and sets in on his lap. He opens it and looks inside.

“A whole box just for pleasure. Some of them are for pain, but even pain brings you pleasure. Doesn’t it?”

I sweep my tongue around my lips and summon the courage to speak. “Yes, Sir.”

“You aren’t just a dirty slut, you’re a pain slut.”

“I like when you tell me to hurt myself.” I suck on my thumb while we look at each other.

“Dirty pain slut. Grasp the ring attached to the right nipple clamp and pull it a little while I decide what I want to see next.”

I hook my finger into the ring on the clamp and ease it down, each movement down makes it squeeze tighter. I don't pull it far because the pain is blinding, not arousing.

"Let go," he says, moving toward me with a dildo in one hand, my favorite vibrator in the other.

I drop my hand and the tension eases, back to arousal.

"It's so hard not to touch you," he whispers in my ear as he drops the toys in my lap. I grab them before they roll away. "Speaking of hard." He's back in the chair, grabbing his package, and shaking it.

"Tomorrow I'll explain my reasons," I choke out. "Which first?" I hold up the toys. Back to the task at hand.

The change in topic doesn't phase Taylor, he replies, "Dildo. Fuck yourself for me, Cin."

I drop the vibe to the bed. "I may need lube." A moment of brattiness has grabbed me.

"You're a slut, you're soaked from the pain. Do you need a heavier dose? Pull on the left ring, hard."

"I'm fine. I'll just—"

"Pull on the ring Chloe." He launches himself from the chair and takes two steps toward me.

I glare at him and he catches himself. I tug on the ring, tightening the hold on my sensitive nub. A fresh wave of liquid overflows from my pussy.

We have a battle with our eyes. Taylor dares me to disobey his commands. I wonder what he'd do if I did, what punishment would he come up with? Would it be now or when he could touch me?

I look away first. "Let go." HIs voice is hoarse, strained. Controlled Taylor is not so controlled. Could I make him lose it completely?

I drop my hand and spread my legs, sliding the dildo inside my drenched cunt. I fuck myself with it furiously. It whets my appetite, but it will never satisfy.

I wish Taylor was holding me, kissing me while I do this. But it's my own insipid rules that keep him sitting in my computer chair. I've come so many times in that chair while talking to him.

"Are you going to touch yourself?" I ask, slowing the show of masturbation.

"No. I want to focus on watching your pleasure." His eyes are wide with arousal, fists clenched as his sides. Is he fighting his desire to touch me?

I want him to shove his face in my cunt and lick my clit until I can't move. I want him to drown in my desire.

Admitting that would break my rules. The need makes me groan, but I can pretend it's the way my fingers swirling around my cunt, around the dildo. I gather the dew on my fingers, so I can lick it off, so I can show him what he does to me.

His tongue moves against the air as mine moves against my fingers. I pretend he's licking me.

He looks at his watch. "You should remove the clamps it's been nearly thirty minutes."

"You only paid for a thirty minute session."

"Take off the clamps and make yourself come slut." His brows raise in challenge.

I bite my lip in anticipation of the blood rush to my nipples. It will hurt like hell. I pull one off, the agony makes me howl and I throw myself back, clutching my breast.

"Calm yourself down and roll your nipple between your thumb and finger."

"I can't," I wail.

Taylor is standing over me with a stern face. "You can and you will."

I gulp in some air as the torment slips away. I roll the tender nub as ordered until it feels good.

"Now the other nipple, but grab it as soon as you slip the clamp off."

I hold my breath and pull it free. The blood rushing through burns, my fingers can't grab the teat for several heartbeats, and then finally it catches. I pinch and roll until the spark catches fire in my body.

"Vibrator," he whispers in my ear. I could turn my head and touch him, but I'd be breaking my rules.

I grope at the bed, unable to find the energy to sit or even move my head. Taylor presses it into my hand. I flick the switch on and press it against my clit, unsure if I have the energy to come.

"Maybe next time I'll have you put one of those clamps on your clit."

His words buzz through my body. This is why I love him. The next moment the orgasm slams into me like a meteor, burning, fast, hard, leaving an impact.

I can't stop shaking even after the pleasure dissipates. Taylor's arms come around me, his body presses against mine.

"You're breaking the rules," the words shake off my tongue.

"Paid time is up. I was certain a half hour would be sufficient for you to get off, slut." He strokes my arms and it slows the shudders. Eventually, under his attention, they cease.

"You broke me," is all I can say.

He kisses my neck and shoulders. "Not yet, sugar."

"Sugar?"

"Sugar and spice. Chloe and Cinnamon. You are both, not always at the same time."

"Now what?"

He smiles. "Now it's my turn."

It's A Date

TJ

I stroke Chloe's hair. I want to fuck her. My hard-on is raging, but she's exhausted from everything I pushed and dragged her through. Her hair is sticking to her face from sweat, her heart hasn't slowed to normal, her breaths are too shallow. She needs care not a good fucking.

"Now I get you a snack then a shower if you want it."

"What about you?" She gropes behind her but it's half-hearted.

I grab her arm and press it down against her side. "Chloe, I can tie you to the bed if you can't let me care for you. Don't worry about me."

I kiss her neck. I go to the kitchen and slice an apple. Adding crackers and a couple slices of cheese creates a well-rounded snack. I return to her with the snack and a glass of water.

She's asleep. I set the snack aside and strip my clothes away. My dick is still hard from the Cinnamon experience.

Lying beside her, I stroke the shaft.

I imagine what I wanted to do with her. Order her to her knees to suck me off, fuck her, come inside her, bury my face in her cunt and lick her until she comes.

Everything we did last weekend, I want do them again. And a few new activities. Tie her up, tease her, more impact play; I purchased a new flogger and crop curious about which sensation she will enjoy most.

I let her moans echo in my head, especially from the bathroom at the bar. Her cunt gripped my dick so hard when she came I couldn't stop myself. Calling her a slut turns her on, so did the pain from the clamps. The way her cunt glistened from her arousal, it filled the room and it took all my self control not to dive in and have a taste.

I'm so easy when it comes to her. My cock shudders, and I pump as it spurts pleasure. The warmth of her spice shudders through my body and I can't hold back a moan.

She shifts beside me, and my heart leaps through my body. Did I wake her? She presses her body against mine, her arm coming over me.

I stroke her arm and she sighs contentedly.

I didn't plan on staying the night, but I don't want her to wake alone. First I turn out the light, then set an alarm on my phone early enough to return to my apartment for suitable work clothes. My office's idea of casual Friday is no tie.

I close my eyes for a moment. Pussy shoving her way between our bodies makes me open them. The cat curls up between us and I roll my eyes before setting down again. "I'd complain but I think I'm the one intruding," I say.

The cat is purring. I let the sound lull me to sleep.

Next morning

I wake to my alarm. Chloe swipes her arm up at the noise. I roll over and turn it off. I curl back into her, kissing her neck and shoulders.

"You're still here," she says.

"I didn't want you to wake alone and feel used."

"No?" her voice perks a little.

"No." I kiss down her back, until I find the spot that makes her sigh and wiggle. I blow on the damp skin then kiss my way back up. "Oh my sweet angel." Her sweet ass cradles into my lap as we spoon. Could we stay here forever?

"I'm sorry I crashed—"

I grab skin between my teeth. "Do not be sorry. I ambushed you showing up. I needed to see you and I thought it would be a good way to keep your boundary."

Chloe thrusts her shoulder against me. "I guess it didn't violate my polices. I don't—"

To get her attention, I bite her again. "I have to tell you something."

"What time is it?"

I smack her ass. "Listen, Chloe."

She sniffs. "I'm listening."

"Under duress. There is something you need to hear." I roll her to her stomach and kiss up her spine. "I love you.

She tries to roll over but I hold her down. "Don't say anything, don't move. Just enjoy." I nip at her shoulder, then kiss from her bicep to her wrist. I suck the soft skin of her inner wrist into my mouth and she gasps.

"Tay—"

"I love the way you moan, the way you come, the way you gasp when I give you a command. I wanted to tell you before I have to leave." With a sigh I roll away to check the time. Is there enough time to tease her? When I move back to kiss her good morning, she slides her hands to my dick.

Fuck yes, I suppose there is.

"I will need a morning quickie," she says stroking me.

My cock is instantly hard. Whatever my girl needs I will provide. I part her thighs and find her slick, ready for me. There's quick and there's instant; I want the former. I stroke her clit with my thumb until her nails dig into my shoulders.

She rolls to her side, pressing back her butt nestles into my belly. My cock nudges between her legs. She's so slick, so ready for me I slip in. I wrap my arm around her and stimulate her clit while I move inside her. She moves with me, her body gripping me despite the liquid.

That's all it takes to push me over the edge. I've fucked her so many times and after it seems as if I want her more than before we started. I am insatiable, and not just the sex, I love being around her.

Deep inside her I shudder a release, but I keep going until it's too painful to move. Then I slow my touches on her clit until I'm brushing, teasing. "Can you come like this?" I tease her ear with my mouth.

She shakes her head, her hips rocking as she tries to get more friction. "Harder, please."

"Beg. Beg me to hurt you." I scrape my teeth across her shoulder.

"God, I love when you hurt me," she moans, her back arching. "Hurt me, TJ. Make me come, Sir."

She's a fucking Goddess. "You know what I'd love to do? Put the clover clamp on you here." I pinch her clit.

She cries out and I sink my teeth into her shoulder. I would love to draw blood but we haven't discussed that limit. I rub the squeezed clit between my fingers, making her squirm against me.

"That's my girl. Come for me." I soothe her with some gentle flicks of my finger as her thighs clamp against my hand. The muscles under her skin ripple as her throat pours out a song of pleasure.

I drop my head against hers as our bodies slow and cool.

After a while she groans and stretches. "I don't want to leave this bed."

I nuzzle her. "Me neither."

"I'm tempted to call out of work. I haven't missed a day in months."

"That is rather tempting." I flip my head to the side, my heart picking up pace.

She rolls over and grabs her phone. Her eyes stick to mine as she speaks to her boss in a weak voice. "Too sick to come in. I don't want to pass this on to anyone else." She's a good actress, and it makes me wonder if she's cultivated her skill from acting on camera.

I hold my breath until she hangs up and I call in myself, but I'm less tense. My boss doesn't give a fuck.

When I'm done, I roll her to her back, kissing her deeply. "We're free for three days."

"I guess drinks tonight are out." I notice a hint of disappointment in her voice. We haven't been out at all. I've been treating her like Cinnamon because I can't keep my hands off her or my dick out of her. But she needs romance, she needs to know I want her outside the bedroom.

"Let's go out tonight. What sounds good? Dinner and a movie? Dancing and drinks?"

"Dinner and drinks."

I brush my lips over her her eyes and cheeks. "You won't get me drunk and take advantage of me will you?" I rest my forehead against hers, enjoying the moment.

She rubs her nose against mine, which is also her shaking her head. "Tay?" her voice is a whisper. Her body is tense.

I roll away from her and turn her to her belly. I bite her shoulder. "Chloe, my sweet Chloe." I brush her hair to the side and kiss the back of her neck. My lips travel down her spine, my tongue darting out to taste her salty skin. I stop at her lower back and kiss across to her hip. I grab her ass with my hands, pressing hard into her muscle.

My lips move back up her body until she's limp and primed. I lay body across hers, pressing her down with my weight. I tease the outer shell of her ear. "Sweet Chloe, I never told you how you make me feel."

"No." She isn't tense.

"I love you Chloe."

"You don't want Cinnamon?" she gives voice to her fears. Has her worry been building in her the whole time?

"Cinnamon is an aspect of you. If pretending you are someone else helps you during sex, that's fine. It's you who I want. All of you. The sexy slut and the sweet good girl."

My dick stirs against her leg, and I ignore it. I can't help how she turns me on.

"I've been afraid to love you. Afraid that you still had feelings for Sherry." She buries her face in my shoulder. "I love you so much Tay. All the times we cried together and laughed. We've shared so much." Her voices cracks and her body jerks.

I draw back to look at her face and I realize she's crying. My hands cradle her face. "Oh sweet angel. You are my best friend. You've been my everything since—when I needed you." I roll to my back and tug her so I can hold her. She crawls between my legs, her head on my chest, still sobbing.

"I'm not unhappy, just overwhelmed," she manages.

I stroke her hair thinking of everything we've done, everything I've demanded of her, and she's risen to every challenge. Has it been too much? "I've been a selfish Dominant, only using you for what I needed, what I wanted. I haven't been mindful of your wants."

She rubs her cheek against my chest, wiping the tears away. "I wanted everything we've done Taylor. I was the one who demanded you make good on all your promises the first weekend."

"I let you over extend yourself for my selfish whims. And then I sprung my deep feelings on you when you were vulnerable."

She pulls away, the tears of overwhelm replaced with lightning. I've unleashed a storm and here comes the thunder. "I am an adult. I can make my own choices. If I have a hard time after that's my problem, not yours. You might top me, but I'm still capable of saying yes or no to you. Right? If I said donkey or stop, you'd stop?"

"Yes. You are right." I squeeze her. "I hate when you are hurting."

She relaxes again and my heart constricts. I want to take care of her, but I can take it to extremes. Something Sherry and I fought about more than once.

I kiss Chloe's head.

"Can I tell you something?" she asks. "About why I won't rely on you for money."

My heart leaps. Yes. "Please."

"You know I have an older sister."

"Yes."

"She got married just after college. And she got pregnant right away and quit her job. Her husband turned out to be an ass and she was screwed for a couple years. I was still in high school when it happened, and it was pretty horrifying. It's not personal, but I don't want to be in a position where someone else can control me. Or fuck me over. I mean if something happens I'll be fucked up emotionally, but losing my ability to take care of myself will fuck up my life."

She twists in my arms so she can look up at me. "I hope you understand. I can give you more details."

I pull her closer. I want to assure her I'd never do something that could fuck her over. But I know better. Even what seems like the best relationship can break. "I want to say I'd never do that, but I never thought I'd get dumped months before my fucking wedding. So we'll figure things out." I cover her hand with mine and lace our fingers.

"I love you," she says her face still tipped up to mine. "I'm sorry I freaked out."

"I'm sorry I wanted to fix it and stopped the cleansing."

"We should get up, shower and eat. Were you serious about going out tonight?"

"Do you want to go out?" She deserves to be treated like the angel she is.

"I'd like that." She smiles, relaxed, happy.

Guilt punches me in the gut. "I should have asked you earlier but I couldn't keep my hands off you. I don't know if I can manage tonight."

"Nothing I didn't want. I was the one who dragged you into that bathroom." She lifts our hands and kisses my fingers.

"Then I bent you over the sink and called you my dirty slut."

She groans and stretches. "That was so fucking hot, Tay. I used that so many times to get off."

My dick flexes. "You are a dirty slut."

She smirks. "I am your dirty slut."

I wiggle out from under her once my feet are on the floor I pick her up. "Come on then dirty girl, you need to get clean."

Perfect Date

Chloe

We can't keep fucking every minute of the day. But every time I look at Taylor across the table from me I imagine his head between my legs, licking my pussy like it's his first and last meal.

I reach over and run my index finger over the back of his hand holding his fork. He gives me a smile and I crook my finger at him, urging him closer.

We lean in and I whisper. "I can't stop thinking about you going down on me."

"This is supposed to be a romantic dinner." He drops his fork.

"My panties are soaked."

He wipes his face with the white cloth napkin from his lap. He pulls his chair closer. "Go to the bathroom and remove them."

My eyes are wide for a moment. Taylor's expression doesn't change. He's serious. I push back from the table and grab my purse from the back of my chair. I wind through the crowded restaurant. Inside one of the stalls I remove my panties. I press them against my nose to breathe in what Taylor does to me before shoving them in my purse.

I cannot get enough of him. Even though I should be angry at the way he pushed the boundaries of our relationship when he came over for his private show, I'm not. That night was way too fucking hot. A new rush of desire flows as I remember how hard I came.

My thighs are sticky as I make my way back to our table. The air in the restaurant cools my exposed skin. The stubble was bothersome, so I shaved today but I left a landing strip for Taylor.

As I'm walking, I see a familiar face. I take a detour, praying she hasn't seen me. Tori Adams from my office. She fucking hates me after I screwed up giving her a message. My asshole boss forgave me, so she should be over it. But she's not and if she sees me my life is over. I can't even glance over my shoulder.

She's in a different part of the restaurant, so as long as I don't use the washroom again, I should be fine. I don't mention her presence to Taylor as I slide into my seat and eat without comment.

"Give your purse, Cinnamon."

I hesitate, but his eyes tell me that's a bad idea. I hand it over and he opens it out and removes my panties. He shoves them in his pocket and spends a minute fondling them. "Your panties are always wet, my pet. Perhaps you should stop wearing them." He doesn't even whisper this, just speaks it across the table. I look around to see if anyone else noticed. No one has so I relax.

He gives me a pointed look "Finish eating. I'm done.

"Me too," I say. I want him more than the food. "I'm ready to go home."

"We aren't going home, sweetheart." His voice promises anything but endearment.

"Where are we going?"

"Maybe a movie. I was pondering the possibility of a dark theatre corner where we couldn't get caught."

My eyes widen and I look around.

"Maybe you'd like to get caught. Maybe someone can watch you blow me or watch while I finger your pussy. You like being watched."

My pussy clenches. It was a large part of the appeal of cam work. I like being watched.

Taylor smirks, and I recognized the look in his eyes. The TJ look. "If you're a good girl, you'll get that reward licking you wanted. If you're a bad girl, you will be punished."

I want both. I don't know which behavior is the good or bad nor do I care. My eyes slide closed and I take a slow breath.

"I planned a romantic evening. I was going to ignore my instincts, my desires and keep my hands off you. But you teased me."

I drop my eyes to my plate. "I'm sorry, sir."

"We'll see. Are you wet?"

I nod, my eyes on my plate. "Yes." My voice shakes, like a reprimanded child.

"Are you done eating?"

I look at my half eaten plate. I can't imagine eating another bite. "Can we take it to go?"

"Yes." He signals our waiter. After he pays, he holds my arm. His fingers grip my arm tight enough to bruise.

"You got me hard in the restaurant, so you'll have to do something about it," he hisses in my ear as he opens the car door.

I slide into my seat wondering what he means. Once he's in the car, he unzips his pants. I look at the street. It's not busy anymore, but it's not empty. The car is parked in a shadow of a building. He grabs my hand and wraps it around his erection. I'm still looking out the window.

He grabs my head and pulls me to face him. "You like being watched."

"By people who pay for it." My hands shake as I stroke his cock.

He eases his seat back. He presses a thumb into my mouth. "I want your dirty whore mouth on my cock, Chloe."

What if we are seen? I weigh my safe word on my tongue. My eyes flick to the street, finding it empty relieves my anxiety. I get on hands and knees on my seat and wrap my mouth around him.

He groans and leans further back. HIs hand curls in my hair. "That's my good girl. Suck it all the way in."

I gag but for a moment I'm unable to breathe, choking on him. He grips my hair tighter in acknowledgement, his breath comes in gasps.

"I'm going to come."

I pause but then keep bobbing along his cock. He grips my hair harder, fucking my mouth. He pauses at the top and then overflows. I suck on the tip while he finishes. I gulp it down and then sit up. A passing couple slow down, their greedy eyes make me flush hotter. They give us the thumbs up. I return the gesture as my heart pounds against my ribs.

I wipe my hand with the back of my mouth. When I turn to him, Taylor grins at me. He's sitting up already, digging in his pocket for the keys.

"You are a good girl, we need to get home as fast as fucking possible."

If I'm getting the reward I hope for, I hope he bends a few speed limits.

"I was trying so hard to keep my hands off you tonight. Just for a few hours."

"I'm sorry I ruined your plan." A blatant lie; I'm not, because that was fucking hot. "You kept look at me and you look so sexy, I wanted to tease you so you'd take me home faster."

"I don't mind indulging that desire at all. I was trying to be a good boyfriend."

"You are a great boyfriend." I lean my head on his shoulder. It's so strange to attach that term to Taylor. "You're my boyfriend."

He glances at me with a smile. "You're my girlfriend. This morning it felt like I had done nothing but fuck you, I wanted to show you I want more than just sex. Or do you only want me for sex?"

"What if I do?"

"I could get into that?" he grins.

"I love you Tay. And I need you to get me off, my pussy is buzzing."

My shyness is gone now. No trace of modesty after the car scene.

His apartment smells like him. I want to sink into his bed and never fucking leave. I am definitely stealing a shirt when I leave here.

I'm a bona fide Taylor Jude Denn addict. I am so fucked. He flips on the lights, and in my temporary blindness he grabs me and presses me against the back of the door. He kisses me while he flips the lock into place, then pulls my skirt up around my waist.

Dropping to his knees, he looks up at me like I'm a goddess he's about to worship, or I'm a sacrifice he's about to give up to the gods. I can't decide which as he grips my ass with both of his hands, tucking my hips under, pushing my pelvis out.

He murmurs something about beauty and I can't make out all the words behind the blood rushing in my ears. I decide his words are of reverence, and I watch as he runs his tongue along my slit. My clit is peeking out from the hood in my hyper-aroused state. He teases it with his tongue first, then his teeth. My hips try to jerk away from the rougher treatment, but he holds me there to take the lashing.

This should be my reward, but he's intent on teasing me long enough to make it torture. That is pleasurable as well.

I'm wild with need, so close so close. "Suck my clit please," I beg.

He obliges, and I move closer to the edge. I look down at him, his eyes glazed over with joy and love, giving to me like I gave to him in the car. All for my pleasure and I come knowing he wants me like that, so bad he can't control himself.

My body shudders and I grab the door handle then his head, then shoulders. Taylor doesn't stop moving against me, making electricity zap through my limbs. If I touch him, I may electrocute him.

My legs can't hold me. I'm going to fall. "Yellow," I say between gulps of breath.

He pulls back from me, not letting go. "What's wrong?"

"I'm going to collapse. My legs are shaking so hard."

He stops to assess me. "Turn around."

"Bed?" My eyebrows go in different directions.

He stares at me. I turn to face the door. He adjusts my skirt around my waist and then without warning his hand comes down on my ass. "Ow," I squeal.

He slaps me again. "You've been such a good girl you deserve a little pain with your pleasure."

"Thank you."

His hand comes against me steady. I moan with each slap, the sharp pain blossoming through my body. I didn't know I wanted this. Taylor knew, he knows me better than I know myself.

He stops. "My hand is sore and your ass is a beautiful shade of red."

I move away. "Stop," he commands and I freeze. "Put your hands against the door."

What is he doing? More spanking? I hear a camera click. Taking pictures.

"Okay strip that dress off and get your ass on my bed."

"I can't undo the zipper myself."

He pulls the fastener open and I shed the garment with trembling fingers. My knees tremble as I walk down the hall, he's behind me and I keep looking over my shoulder.

It's the first time I've been in his bedroom. In all our years of friendship I've never been in his private space.

His bedroom is smaller than mine. His bed takes up most of the space. I climb on the generic grey and aqua comforter, a couple pillows with non-matching pillow cases. A pile of laundry near the basket. His closet is open and a mess of clothes on the floor.

It smells like Taylor. And I dive into the pillows, rolling around in his scent. Definitely need a shirt that smells like him for the days we don't sleep over.

"It occurs to me," he muses, drawing my attention. I roll to my back and watch him undress, "You were being bad at the restaurant. You need punishment."

I lick my lips. "LIke what?"

"I have an idea." He pulls open the top drawer on the side table. He dangles a pair of clover clamps in front of me. These have a chain between them. "How much money have you spent on sex toys since you found me on the cam girl site?"

"I'm not sure you want to go into finances."

"You were talking torture. I got confused." I give him my best innocent smile.

He drops the clamps on me. "Put those on." *Punished!* I take the clamps and clip them on, with a hiss of pain as each one latches closed.

He tugs the chain to remind that they tighten even more. I hiss up at him. He pulls out a vibrator from the side table. It's not one of those cheap ones. This one vibrates the whole body.

"What are you going to do?" I ask. My voice cracks betraying my nervousness.

"Sit behind you and reward you with an orgasm."

And the punishment? Are the clamps the extent of my penalty? He slides behind me and I rest against him, feeling safe and warm.

He pushes my chin to my chest. "Open your mouth." I part my lips. He puts the chain for the clamps between my teeth. "Hold onto that with your teeth, slut."

I hold it. I'm unable to speak or move my head.

"If you need to safe word, drop it from your mouth, otherwise if you let it drop there will be consequences."

I nod as much as I can without pulling the clamps tighter. He spreads his legs wider, so he can make me open to him. I press my chin to my chest, any little movement will pull the chain and tighten the clamps. If I can control myself, it won't be too bad.

The vibrator comes to life somewhere outside my view. He runs it along my shoulders so I know how powerful it is. It jiggles down my belly and circles my inner thighs. Any more teasing and I will be shaking, but mercifully he presses it between my legs. He uses the edge to part my cunt lips and press the vibrator against my clit.

I close my eyes and focus on my breathing, letting the pleasure sink into my belly. The arousal seems safer there, he can't seal it away.

His hand is in my hair. The gentle tug is a nice touch, but
then he pulls my head back. Fuck, the clamps tighten on my
nipples. I almost drop the chain, to cry out or curse him,
but as my tongue hits the metal, I recall why I can't.
Punishment will be worse if I drop it unless I need to safe
word.

I grunt hard as he swirls the vibrator around my clit.

Fuck fuck.

He drops my head and the release is as shocking as the
tension.

Fuck!

"I fucking love these clamps. I can't wait to watch you
writhe in pain when you remove them." He laughs, a little
cruelty in my ear.

I want to say something, but I'll drop the chain and I'm not
ready to finish yet. I like seeing my limits then having
Taylor guide me past them. He pulls my head back again,
"Nothing to say?" he hisses in my ear.

I shake my head and the clamp tightens again. My mouth
drops open but I catch the chain with my tongue. This is far
harder than it looks.

"Come for me," he croons in my ear. "I want to see you fall
apart."

I relax into the vibrator and breathe while it builds the orgasm. I want to come, I spread my legs a little further.

So close, so close. My inner thighs quiver and I can see them jiggle. He pulls my head back again, and the pain rips through me, followed by intense pleasure. My mouth opens so I can let out a scream. The tension on the chain keeps it against my bottom teeth.

My entire body is shaking and he keeps rolling the vibe against my clit. Tears spring to my eyes as aftershocks rock me. Then he pushes my head down and pulls the vibe away.

I am still lost in the sensations. I'm vaguely aware of him stroking my arms and kissing my shoulders while I come down.

It seems like forever before equilibrium returns. My muscles are limp and I flop against him. He pulls the chain from my mouth.

"You are so fucking sexy. I don't know why I tried to keep my hands off you."

My brain can't form a thought so I wave my hands.

"Time to remove these little things." He stretches my nipple with the clamp. And then pop it comes off and my hand flies to my breast to assuage the pain. I writhe in his lap, just as he wanted, incoherent curses coming from my mouth.

He unclips the other one and white hot pain sears my brain. I squirm away from him, unintentionally.

He climbs out from behind me and covers his body with mine. "What I love about the clamps is how sensitive they leave you." He flicks his tongue over the area and I almost shoot off the bed. I probably would if he wasn't holding me down.

"Fuck," I mutter as he torments my throbbing nipples.

"I was thinking the same thing. I'd like to fuck you. Are you up for it?"

I nod a little.

"Say it. And don't say it to please me. Do you want to be fucked?"

I bite his shoulder. "Yes Sir."

And in one easy movement he's inside me, his weight on me, and it feels perfect. He moves inside me, slowly, then faster, faster, faster. I lift my hips to meet him.

"Do you want the vibe?" he asks.

"No. I need a break before I come again. I like feeling you inside me."

"It feels perfect."

Exactly. He grabs my ass and fucks me, driving to finish. Bliss, if everything goes right I could live this, I could have this every day. Lazy Sunday mornings making love, Friday nights where he ties me to the bed and whips me, Saturdays nights where we go out with the gang and we can't wait to get home so he can fuck me against the front door.

I'll die an early death from all the orgasms, but it will be a blessed life.

"You with me?" he asks. His hands frame my face.

"Sorry, I was in a fantasy."

He kisses me softly. "About what?"

"Us. Like this could work."

"We could. I've been thinking about it as well. I don't know what you envisioned for your future. As long as I've known you, you've dated but nothing serious."

We search each other's face. "I've never met someone who made me want a future. Why doesn't a future with you scare me?"

"Maybe because we are right. Maybe because we will work."

I nod and I know what I need to do. Quit cam work. If I want our relationship to work, I need to commit myself to him fully. For myself, not for him, not for anyone else. This is me.

I don't know how I will pay my rent while following my heart. In this perfect moment it's hard to care.

My smile is bright. "I love you."

"I love you too. Do you want to cuddle on the sofa and watch TV or a movie?"

"I'd like that." A relationship. Everything is perfect.

A Proposition

TJ

She said this could work.

I turn in the seat Im in and shoot my paper ball at the bin on my buddys entryway. Hes likewise an associate, which is valuable.

So whats the issue?

Nothing, that is the issue.

So shes your dearest companion and a dream fuck? You love her, she adores you. She doesnt need you to cover every one of her bills and you have an issue?

Something will turn out badly, Julian. I screwing know it.

Wed her before it does.

Weve just been dating a little while. I cannot request that she wed me. Regardless of whether Ive known her for a really long time. I moan. I don't know.

Its Monday morning. The weekend with Chloe was astonishing. She enlightened me regarding her fantasies. Marriage, kids in the long run. Continue to work, get a superior line of work. I told her I needed marriage, kids, move to suburbia, continue to work.

You have it so terrible, man. I dont think you were into Sherry this hard.

I was way more awful with Sherry when we previously dated. You knew me three years into the relationship. I was likewise a juvenile fuckhead when I began dating Sherry.

Rather than your development now?

I snatch a paper ball off the floor and toss it toward the band. It goes wide and I shrug. That's right, considerably more adult. Like realizing you cannot propose two weeks into a relationship.

You can. If its the right one, Julian counters.

I push up from the seat. I think perhaps move in together first. She cannot bear the cost of her place and Im tired of driving with an erection.

He gestures. Such a lot of development. Its killing me.

My telephone signals in my pocket. Chloe. Its her, I say, prior to hitting acknowledge call. I press the telephone against my ear. Hello darling.

I cannot hear anything from the get go so I rehash the hello. Then, at that point, I hear it, her cry. Shes crying. Monday morning, its not so much as 9 AM. Child, I cannot help you in the event that you cannot tell me whats wrong?

They terminated me.

What? Who? Inept inquiry. Her butt sphincter chief. For phoning in debilitated when she wasnt. Its her main offense, so that should be the issue.

That bitch Tori, she was at the café on Friday. I didnt think she saw me, however she did. Fuck. I cannot trust this. Im so screwed. She wheezes and hiccups.

Put your head between your legs and relax. Well sort this out.

Sort what out? Shes practically shouting. I have lease due in about fourteen days. Im owe fourteen days worth of pay, yet they can keep that. Possibly I can accomplish cam work. Extra shows. Her breathing sounds more like wheezing as she sets up an arrangement.

I can loan you the cash.

No! We discussed this. I can see her pointing her finger at me, her teeth grasped.

Im not giving it to you, it would be an advance until you found a new line of work and afterward you could take care of me. Or on the other hand I could persuade her this evening to move in with me. Its a one room, so when she has a tantrum and proposing to pay a large portion of the lease, its feasible for her, even with just cam work. Accepting she pulls in what Im speculating. If not, shell have another secretary work soon.

She sneezes. OK.

I cannot persuade her on the telephone. It should pause. What about lunch with me? Would you be able to go to my office and well get a light meal to eat?

No doubt. She wheezes.

I check the time. Alright. That several hours. Clear out your work area, take your stuff home, update your resume, email everybody you know and inquire as to whether they are aware of any positions.

She sniffs again and I wish I could kiss and hold her. I can do that. That is acceptable. Much thanks to you Taylor. Im sorry to trouble you at work.

I was simply finding Julian. Finish that stuff then, at that point, go to my office. You can meet Julian and well eat. I love you.

I sink into my office seat and squirm my mouse to wake the PC. Fuck, I got her terminated.

No I didnt, she recommended phoning in wiped out. This is all on her. However, she might attempt to pin it on me. One more obstacle for later I she gets annoyed with me.

OK, right. Sick do that. Much thanks to you.

Divine beings. For what sweet young lady?

Not accusing me.

You are not to blame.

I attempt to work yet I watch out for the clock. Its early afternoon, at last, and she messages me. In the structure.

Come on up. Sick meet you at the front work area. Up she comes and I see as her and kiss her. She looks drained, as shes been crying.

Would you like to meet Julian or would it be advisable for us to eat?

Eat? Im helpless organization. Possibly I should return home.

Well eat. I put my arm around her midriff and anchor her to me.

We go to my beloved shop. Its swarmed yet we track down a table. We sit with our sandwiches. I realize you will think this is excessively quick, however think about moving in with me.

Youre expected to individuals talk me. Let me know Ill get another line of work or something to that effect.

I definitely realize that, yet I need you to move in with me, notwithstanding. Your place is excessively costly.

You are correct, its excessively quick.

Im ready for this contention. Weve just been screwing two or three weeks, yet weve known one another for a really long time. We dont need to get to know one another, as different couples. We are a level ahead.

When the cloudiness wears off, we probably won't care for one another that much, she counters, pointing her soup spoon at me. I watch the soup trickle off the edges. It looks great, I figure I ought to have requested that.

That is simply it. We may be in a dimness of desire, however we definitely realize we like each other past the sex. You are my dearest companion and presently my sweetheart. We dont need to choose now. I told Julian toward the beginning of today Id wed you if you would consent to it.

That is excessively quick. Im not prepared to get hitched.

Im not asking you. Just to quick advance and go to the living respectively arrange quicker than most couples do. We like one another.

I will consider it. Not just in light of the fact that I have three months before Im screwed. Furthermore, there will be conditions. Like I pay a large portion of the lease despite the fact that you make a fuckton more than me. Also, Im not tidying up after you.

I dont need a house keeper. I need you to be in my bed so I can turn over and screw you as opposed to driving across town.

She feigns exacerbation. I live eight streets away. You could stroll there quicker than driving in busy time.

Whatever conditions you want. I tidy up after myself.

Another eye roll, she might pay for those later. I saw your heap of clothing on the floor close to your hamper.

She has a point. Sick cook for you.

On the off chance that I dont get a substitution line of work in the following fourteen days. Sick need to think about it. she looks tormented by this discussion.

I need you there in light of the fact that I love you not on the grounds that I need to save you. On the off chance that you hadnt lost your employment, I likely would have requested that you move in the following month, in any case. I need you in my life morning and night.

I have one months lease saved. It would be all the more however the entire lease increment screwed me over that way. I need to give one months notice to empty so it very well may be sketchy.

I will get you if you fall.

She snarls at me. She doesnt need to fall or be gotten. Its past the point of no return, shes fallen, she doesnt need to let it be known.

What clothing would you say you are wearing?

I don't know. Would you like to see it?

Indeed I do, yet that will begin something I can't wrap up. Then again a grin creeps onto my face.

No my hot to run little whore. I mean yes I do, however I dont have time.

One of us needs to work I presume.

I snatch her hand and we both get to our feet. Lets leave. She allows me to haul her out of the structure. In the road I glance around. Where would we be able to go for protection?

Screw it, my vehicle is the best well get. A couple of moments calm walk, I open the traveler entryway and hang tight for her to enter. Once inside, I hang over and snatch her ear cartilage with my teeth. I nibble until she shouts out.

How was wiping out your work area?

Awkward. That bitch stopped by and bragged. She didnt say anything, however she remained outside my office for like thirty seconds gazing at me with a smile all over.

Screw it, you despised your work. You are gone. Youll find something better. What's more, youll move in with me. Or on the other hand Ill move in with you or well find something better.

That is the reason we left so quick?

No. You were prodding me. I need you to purchase a collar first. You will wear it until you get a new line of work. Second, I need you to make me dinner. I unfasten a couple buttons of her top and slip my hand inside. I change her areola. Last, return home and make yourself come. In any case, I need you to video it for me.

She moans. Alright.

I bother her areola by brushing my palm over the hard stub. I haul my hand out and start the vehicle. She fastens her shirt then her head gobbles up. I cannot buy a collar.

I pull my wallet from my pocket and two or three twenties on her lap. For the collar and anything you want for dinner.

She checks out the cash. Her mouth opens and closes. She needs to contend, however shes torn. She should be parsimonious at this moment. In any case, I need her to give more idea than just to her nearby requirements. I need accommodation.

I rub the rear of her head then, at that point, snatch her hair. Inclining in faintly, I give my interest. Submit Chloe. Allow me to assume responsibility now.

She gestures a bit. Her eyes drop to her hands laying on her lap. Sick attempt, Taylor.

Im doing whatever it takes not to take your freedom. Youll have some work again soon. You can generally accomplish more cam work. Sick give you space for it. Or then again during the day.

She shakes her head. I need to stop.

What? Why? My hand drops and I pull back to my own space. I havent asked her for that. I dont need to take that from her if she appreciates it. You dont need to stop for me.

Its me. She pulls her eyes from mine.

I hang tight for her to clarify. I check out the clock, I really want to return.

On the off chance that Im going to be with you, I need to be with you. I need to be yours. Just yours. Nothing bad about proceeding, however it doesnt feel right to my heart.

I gesture and stroke the rear of her head. OK. Would we be able to discuss this around evening time? Somewhat more profound. I want to return to work.

Her eyes dart back to mine, her tongue wetting her lips. No doubt. This evening. Sick cook something for you.

What's more, make me a video. One I can use as jolt off feed when I cannot see you.

You might have recorded any of my cam shows.

That wouldnt have been correct. Will you do this for me? I maneuver the vehicle into traffic. I cannot stand by any more extended to get back to my office. Indeed, even my supervisor has limits.

Sick make you a video, TJ. Sir.

Great young lady. Sick prize you for it, later.

She wraps the cash up her satchel. Dont neglect: get the collar first. I need that in the video. Food then my video.

I wont neglect. What time would you say you are taken care of business once more?

Five-thirty. Sick text you when I go home. Surrender you a heads. I ought to be there between quarter to six and six.

At the workplace, I kiss her hard on the mouth. Sick see you around six. I love you. Dont fail to remember your three errands. Id hate to rebuff you.

It would be something awful. We share a grin. I love you as well. Sick be a decent young lady and finish every one of my positions. What's more, Ill attempt to finish my resume today.

She leaves the vehicle and heads for hers. I return to my office. Julian is sitting tight for me. Wheres your young lady? I figured I could meet her.

Shes really regretting life. I gave two or three assignments to divert her. Also, compel her to present a bit. Make me dinner, finish her resume. Stuff like that. I havent given Julian full subtleties of our relationship. The accommodation, the cam work, the ready to take care of business subtleties. That is for Chloe and I.

Possibly toward the end of the week well get some R&R or something like that.

Of course, youll likely phone in wiped out again so you can screw her the entire day and avoid drinks.

I shrug. At the point when you see her youll get why.

Youre in adoration. I know why.

I'm. I give him a grin. Youre simply desirous I tracked down my beauty queen and youre alone.

Im not hoping to submit. You search that poo out.

I do. I figured I would wed Sherry. Presently I figure I will wed Chloe. I can't help thinking about what sort of ring she needs.